PERPENDICULAR
PRONOUN

PerpendIcular Pronoun

MONOLOGUES

Adrian Hart

S

Sophia Publishing

Perpendicular Pronoun

2/23 Victoria Avenue
Whanganui
New Zealand
First published by Sophia Publishing
Perpendicular Pronoun
ISBN: 978-0-473-58412-2

S

Adrian Hart

Table of Contents

Perpendicular Pronoun

Who are you? I ask myself with impertinent familiarity of my silent addressee, silent in your magnificent and impenetrable clarity, your intimate distance, your absence made of paradise, your youthful truth as unknowable even to yourself but as intractable as a fact of nature. Who is this unnameable you, wherever you are, whether you exist or not, whether someone or no one, nothing or everything, Goddess or mortal, from the past or the future, you whom I knew before I first saw you and was only waiting for you to find me out? Again, who are you, and why do you refuse to reply and alleviate the assaults of my affection? I ask with such emphasis only because naively turning to myself and asking 'Who am I ' in isolation from all other questions would only lead me down an endless rabbit hole of unanswerable questions. How can I say what I am if I am devoid of self, a protesting, florid hysteric, unable to speak with any presumption or authority of my own, if I have become unknowable to myself, my own enigma, a 'forgotten sphinx in the desert?' The moment, for example, I even posit this *I*, what would seem such a perpetual point of reference vanishes into the air, reduced to a mere zero point of departure, to no more than a direction determined only by my search for you. After all, the first person subject needs its corresponding second person object if it is to be termed as such. And yet if I maintain a discreet and dramatized distance from my own undoubted hypocrisy and insipidity, if I view my interior landscape from the outside as I would a passing landscape of fields and mountains, consciousness might redeem the untranscendable, impossible horizon of this *I* and I might at least maintain an elegant modicum of dignity. Even if you do not listen to me perhaps I can at least forgive myself troubling heaven's deaf ears with this rambling repost to the world, this investigation of silent nothingness addressed to no one but the night's void, to this unnamable muse of no address. I might at least discover what it is I am trying to say and these investigations will sooner than later lead me somewhere beyond this dark thicket and into higher, open spaces. I can only try not to lose my way or lose the plot, as I may well do, as I almost certainly will, I can only try not to tie myself in those knots of confusion in which grammar, with its endless tussle between subject and object, likes to entrap us, as I toy with words and they in turn with me in their own cat and mouse game, a game I must inevitably loose. But as language is by definition social and always knows me better than I do, even a ruminating, chattering internal monologue cannot articulate itself without external reference and signification. The inquiry must inevitably run into an impassable cul-de-sac if there is no no one to whom I can speak, no one to prevent me from tumbling into gibberish. Unlike Oedipus, I can't solve your impossible riddle, I can't erase the enigma of your inaccessible darkness, I can't blindly pretend you don't exist in the hope of defending a nonchalant normality. Barely confident enough to invest plausible reality to the perpendicular pronoun I call myself, who am I, despite this delirium which overtakes me like a fever, to dismiss you as a mere fiction, a phantasm of my own making? If speaking to oneself is the first sign of madness, then if I speak nonsense I may at least with the aid of Socratic detachment pay attention to such nonsense. I am sabotaged by language the moment I speak, what I say distorted in the saying, but even if there are things I am unable to say because unutterable, then perhaps by not uttering them I can utter them and by not expressing the inexpressible I can express it. Perhaps, after all, silence is impossible without speech, without noise. Perhaps silence is not closed but opened by the very failure of speech, by having to speak and say the things we don't mean. Yes, I think I will stage myself, as is the Italian way, with that irony necessary for the effective expression of both love and anger, knowing well that how we appear on the world's public stage usually reflects our true self more than the figure we present in the unguarded privacy of our homes.

Perhaps you emerged from the transcendent into the temporal realm in the same way an immortal will choose on occasion, even out of curiosity, to holiday in the more dramatic world of the mortals only to know what it is to be a human. You, who understand everything from the viewpoint of a beatific eternity and for whom the soul is here only for its own joy, often laugh at my unhappiness, and I agree, there is nothing funnier, but perhaps your apparent silence is a gentle, graceful provocation, perhaps, indirectly and finally, you are telling me that it is through you that I will see myself. Even if my own silent dialogue with myself could be of no earthly interest to you, practicing indifference to you would be useless, for what good would that do if me if, like truth, you stood before me, cold and naked, not caring whether I recognized you or not? What then does my encounter with you reveal other than that I am unknowable to myself? But you live easily and fearlessly with the unknown, without my own stupid appetite for certainty. Can I face the unknown without fear, in the way one is not necessarily diminished but, on the contrary, infinitely enlarged by contemplating the magnitude of the universe in the night sky? What does it matter if I do not know who you are or who I am if you, more than truth or knowledge, are yet their very opening, the very light by means of which the universe understands itself? You confront me with in the dead end of my own finitude, you release me from the deadly weight of the already known, from the knowledge which enslaves as much as any mood, you are the barely recoverable other world of a gentler time, the opening to the possibility of a future beyond the world of the merely measurable. How can I now settle for anything less? I would only be half of myself, only partly born, if I did not investigate this thoroughly, bring forth the unknown from obscurity, clarify and elucidate and reclaim these hidden, flirtatious, seductive truths floating around me like birds of paradise. Whether you be Goddess or muse, my guide leading me away from error and desolation into the clear skies of the absolute, or simply an enchantress leading me to rack and ruin, I don't know, but out of the emptiness which produces all things an animated chain of impressions and associations invade my private, internal theatre and seek to connect with one another in a grand conclusion: unsolved questions and surmises, thousands of vaguely lucid thoughts organically multiplying and coalescing around themselves, a ragbag assemblage of notions and images, narratives following the tropes and plot complications of novels, films, operas or soap operas, memories of famous quotations, samplings of literary sayings, truisms, platitudinous observations, snippets of would-be wisdom, sagacious sayings from the East, a vague miasma of metaphysical, ethical, social, scientific or aesthetic associations. Yes indeed, love, like pain, makes philosophers of us all and, as if a stranger to myself, it is I who have become the very object of my enquiry. The personal also becomes impersonal, the particular universal. Everything now shouts at me: You have had your fun with all your dissonant chords, now show me this vital, laughing, happy resolution before Mr Death, the officious little fellow of little account, has his last say. The situation is all surely too vague, as it stands it is too unsatisfactory aesthetically, ethically and spiritually. Love, surely more than a vague and useless melancholy, is also a mode of understanding, and if I do not wish to be the slave of my own passions I am bound to understand them, so I will climb what they call the ladder of love, I will become its Alpine explorer, a climber of vertical slopes, of great heights, or even perhaps an airplane pilot ascending from the clouds of earthbound obscurity to touch the brilliant skies of you, my unfathomably transparent absolute, and only then might I one day come to learn something.

My first meeting with her was predictably catastrophic, as all such meetings are, yet I cannot reproach her for so pulling the ground from under me. If I once mocked the world, how can I now mock a world from which she rose and to which she lends her special beauty? Who am I, who do I think I am, this mere daydreaming, haunted house of a soul, this bustling theatre of sensations, to harbor bitterness against its very existence, to doubt its very foundation, its very whys and wherefores? I have long passed that crucial stage in life when you realize that you are not the royal monarch at the centre of the universe you fancied you were, not the centre around which everything revolved. It was long ago that, seeing myself in a mirror, I mistook myself for a knowable unity, even if I sensed there was yet a blind spot, not recognizing that I was hidden from myself, that this blind spot was none other than my own self bending and warping like a black hole everything around it? My own mind recognizes itself and rejoices in its unknowing and I have no doubt the world has its own reasons for existing and doing what it does, as she perhaps has her own reasons for behaving likewise. Who am I to question the world simply because it does not present itself in a neatly bound package of explanations, who am I to say that it should not have been in the first place, that it is a horrible mistake, that there is only chance and no order in this world and it is all a shabby, inelegant chaos? That the universe came into being through a random, capricious loss of symmetry at the initial stage of its birth with the big bang might also suggest that we too are all resting on nothing, on the slightest of insubstantial, floating probabilities and possibilities. It sometimes only seems absurd because of our inability to master it, because we see only a few lines, imperfect and incomplete, of the written drama to which we are conscripted. The world, like me, is itself incomplete, unfinished business, a work in progress. No, again, I have no quarrel with it as I have no quarrel with her. And yet are we not both already beyond the world and its dirty tricks? It is said that a joke is a tiny revolution, a mental shortcut, an instantaneous jump from A to Z, and it seems together we are our own joke on the world at its expense, an elusion of its treacherous antimonies, a liberation from its death march. The energy so released when the ground is so torn from under our feet is our relief, our secret. If it is a trick of nature, of human biology, if it happens despite me then I gladly consent to its deceit. If I was once afraid of love's infection, and my attraction to her is the pathogen of this disease, then she is its vaccine, and thus, forever immune from pain, even when she is absent I have only to say her name and she reappears before me.

Why have you been so stupid, what do you see in her, why do you read into her things that aren't there, why do you want to see her when she is so clearly unsuited to you? they asked me after they saw us together on the beach a few days ago. But love, not so stupid, has its own fine wit, and I would only reply that sometimes in our ventures we must do a thing to discover the reason for it, and it is she, the witty questioner and deflator of my hypocrisy, who has awoken me from my stupor, it is she who has untied the knot that I had become and made me infinitely less blind, less stupid and illiterate in the ways of the world. The traitor within could judge me, seed Mephistophelian doubt, forensically analyse my motivations, question me forever in an infinite cycle, but enough, there are limits after all and she, if anyone, almost by definition, is surely beyond and above all such meagre limits. When she or anyone else, perhaps tempting me, asks me why it is I think I love her, how can I answer when any answer would clearly be wrong, the very answer her betrayal? Is it not a matter of loving someone not for this or that reason, for this or that quality, but of loving such indivisible, indescribable, incomprehensible qualities precisely only because one loves? Reckless, fatuous in my venture I may be, but to read we must first learn to spell, and is not love always excessive, a passionate faith rather than a parsimonious act of economy done in the hope of any return? And rather than any frivolous diversion is not my interest in her also contemporaneous and indivisibly bound to my endless search for the absolute itself, even if this absolute should constantly disappear into nothingness like a quantum particle at the moment it comes into being, evading me at the very instant I try to define it? It seems that our meeting is historically necessary, that we are the playthings of eternity, that the fates are intransigent and it is beyond my power to do anything about them, and this moment is what the years behind me have been carrying me toward, their culmination, their massive accumulating chord. It it is surely more interesting and less mundane to surmise that perhaps the universe is its own poetic romance, that somewhere in the heart of things there is indeed a clandestine order, a destiny unbeknown to us, and that somewhere or somehow, invisibly behind the staged visibility of random phenomena, in retrospect it would make some kind of heavenly and blatantly obvious sense with an inevitability as elegant and precise as a mathematical law of nature. I might, following such scientific analogy, even find myself in accord with the scientists and mathematicians for whom this universe composed of discretely ordered and mathematically measurable quanta and of no obvious practical application is by no means the miasma of meaningless chaos today's absurdists like to think it is. Observe how everything is calibrated and in its own place down to each minuscule detail: molecules, microbes, genomes, cells, chromosomes, virions, metabolic pathways, DNA code, atoms, electrons, protons, nuclei, quarks, nuons, quantum fields and fluctuations, all that of which our own selves and this world of supposedly solid, all too solid matter are composed. Its elements refer to each other within their own celestial context as though written and encoded on some giant blackboard in simultaneous time, spelling out... What? What, exactly, could they be spelling? The Grand Unified Theory, The

Theory of Everything, the very E=MC2 of the spirit, of love itself? But despite any speculation, no matter what science discovers, the structure of the atom, like everything else, will surely resist all final analysis and the sea's waves still roll endlessly towards me, drowning all the old contradictions and antinomies, still murmuring that there is more in store for us in this grand enterprise than we ever knew what to do with. That is what I see and read in her. Everything that has already been said and will be said, everything that needed to be said is already written in her face and in her nature and, in the end, all I can do and say, if I can at least say one true and intelligent thing, is tell her I love her. It is indeed the simple thing that is hardest to do. And praise, of course. Praise, that's all I can do in the end, praise and sing like a dog to the moon, nothing else.

The celebrities, the prominent, the technicians who make life more convenient, those who write articles about things, they put me in the shade with their endless industry. They have plenty to say and show for themselves, they say there is work to be done, that time is running out and we must act and go forward, they understand, connect, systemize, plan, engage and converse. And what do I have to show and say for myself? Nothing. But what interest do I have for all this now when I am lost to the world and can only think of her?

I have become too parochial and comfortable in this place, I have become so finite to myself and so lacking in the liveliness of the indefinite that I am in danger of turning into stone. I am a self yet nobody I recognize and without even a part on this provincial stage to call my own. I know that I am not as complete as I would like to believe, I know that I am missing something, but perhaps I only have myself to blame. Perhaps in my search for quietude I have excluded myself from too much of the world, perhaps this quietude has come at too great an expense. Apparently I have everything I need yet I am dying of ennui with one eye on this death clock, forever prevaricating and procrastinating. I do do nothing of any ultimate or local consequence, my thoughts spin in endless circles with barely a diary or journal to account for myself. No, it's really got to stop. I should do something about it. Perhaps it's time I traveled again? After all, I haven't been out of the country for ten years or so. Yes, this time let's decide once and for all. I will travel, I will throw myself into the world's vast realms of possibility and remind myself once again of the Great Unity of Being. It isn't enough to play the fool to myself, it's time to see the world again rather than read about it in books and newspapers or see it on the screen, it's time to remind myself that the world beyond these constricted borders exists without me. Yes, I have become insular, quite the country bumpkin. Epidaurus, Delphi, Venice, Paris, London, Milan, Florence, Salzburg, Vienna, Prague, Hong Kong, Auckland. I went to those places years ago, even if I had already seen and known most of them in my own mind's eye long before stepping foot in them, but I want the thrill of falling again into that vertigo of time and place known to all travelers, especially when today one can change places and time zones in a matter of days or hours. But first to Paris for a week or two. Because I never truly got to know this city I have unfinished business there. Yes, I will travel, even if I must endure today's airports which look more like shopping malls and where the flight itself is only one other adjunct to the commodities on sale, but I am sure, at the very least, that I won't be bored.

Paris, yes, I am here at last, I took the journey, the 11th arrondissement, near Église Saint-Ambroisea and a quick walk away from Le *Cimetière du Père-Lachaise.* Three weeks. But as you would expect, Parisians and tourists, like everyone everywhere, peering down at their mobile phones, handbags for sale everywhere you look, the ubiquitous logos and brands. It is too eerie. What has happened since I last came, why have people changed? What do people talk about here? The everyday practicalities, business, making money? Anyway, it's almost impossible to talk to anyone nowadays, what with everyone living in their own head. It's as though in speaking to you they somehow risked compromising themselves or betraying a secret. I'm here too, I'm one of them, even if only as a tourist, but what would I be doing if I lived here? Working in a shop, or with a public relations company like nearly everyone else nowadays? Who knows? How could you fall in love here now, in the way people once did in this city of romance? But, of course, this is nonsense. They still fall in love, somehow or another, I am sure, even in their own modern way, and I am merely merely nostalgic for a city I only imagined and never knew in the first place.

No, I have all the riches in the world except, perhaps... except what? I am in a hotel. Why am I in a hotel, of all places, why did I come to this city anyway, what was I thinking? To see the world? But she is not here and all I see in my mind is her face and sometimes, pathetically, I even mistake someone in the street for her.

My own history doesn't begin with the time of my own birth but merely continues the thread from where things had previously left off, as I can tell simply by reading the letters and looking at the old pictures of my ancestors. A good enough life then, I admit. Born, first memories, nothing out of the ordinary, mustn't complain. Nameless until given a name, my name. Then a table under which I crawled, hid under it and made of it a little house, harpsichord music on the radio. was it Bach or Palestrina or Rameau? A passing Morris Minor, the young neighbourhood girl who looked after me, the couple I called Uncle and Auntie across the street. A few local details then, some local colouring. Any traumas? No doubt, but I can't remember and certainly I can't for the life me think of anything worth writing home about. All this of interest only as anchors to the ocean bed of the past. And oh yes, I had a large peddle car made of metal, and a Prussian blue overcoat I wore in the snow and wind. But what home was this? If I had stayed there, at that place, what would have happened, what would I have become at the age of twenty, thirty, forty, sixty? Yet, despite that, here I am, by an act of fate on the other side of the world.

Mundane thoughts to follow: Is she, for instance, eluding me because she does not truly feel anything for me the way she claimed she did that luminous day a few months ago, or is there someone else less dull, someone perhaps less fatally flawed? I believe there is, oh yes, and I think I know who it is all right. Why else doesn't she come and see me, why doesn't she call, what is it I have said, what is it I did or did not do? I ask, like a detective or barrister. It is not as though I were openly pursuing her. Is there something wrong with me? Perhaps I am too old for her. Or is it simply that he has money? Is that it then, is that all it comes down to? What is it she sees in him, of all people? What special qualities does he possess that I don't? She says in her angrier moments that I am vain and self-centred but, surely, is there anyone more so than this fellow? No, he is surely more in love with his expensive new Audi than with her. But worse than that he is the sort I know too well, the sort who tells a truth in the service of a lie and for whom a thing exists only if it is measurable and can fit on a spreadsheet. Does she even love him as, in one drunken moment, she claimed she loved me? Yes, or on the other hand perhaps this jerk was perhaps her own way of bringing me closer to her, perhaps it was her intention to seed jealousy in me. That could be it. But that she could live happily without me is unthinkable. How is it possible that someone else could be the bearer of this happiness other than my own self, for whom it was proffered to me with my own name on it? Yes, it was only when he appeared on the scene that I knew that through some diabolical plot he might steal her from me. Yet one more reminder how conditional such love is, one more reminder of how the most important things are often hidden precisely because of their familiarity, how the nearest so often seems the furthest. Yes, jealousy, that other, more malign virus: could it be as brutal and vulgar as that, and she is now merely an object of exchange, a trophy, a prize in a competition I have lost? Already beginning to doubt my own intentions, I am tempted to surrender the fight and gallantly renounce her, I am ready to play the civilized non-aggressor rather than the vainglorious winner, retreating defeated but virtuous, the convenient, sacrificial beast. On the other hand she, along with everyone else, would of course despise me, but I am damned if I am to play the jealous Caliban, the resentful watcher of other's joys; no, I am not to be reduced to a crank grumbling to himself inside his own head, I don't want any part of this operatic threesome, I refuse to turn all this into mere breathless drama and theatre, I won't play the third person in this vicious, deadly triangle. It is unnecessary, irrelevant, a futile disturbance and it's time I decided what I finally want for myself, if it can be said that I can know what I want when desire is the issue. After all, it is all about that complicated word love and shouldn't that be the very beginning and end of the matter? Nevertheless, something does indeed call for a resolution, such as marriage, perhaps. But would she ever marry me? Marriage would bring a certifiable certainty, such a public declaration could rid me of this febrile romanticism and reverse the ruin, it could bring me down to earth again. This would perhaps be the solution to this aesthetic and quasi-religious quandary, a means of squaring and taming this triangle. Yes, risking everything, I should put my cards on the table and my money where my mouth is, even if she might laugh at me and I would be nowhere again and back to square one.

To loose you is also to find you, and even if it seems that I am then nothing without your presence, my very own nothingness is yet my everything and mine to give, the hollowed darkness of my own self its own light. To seek is to suffer and to seek nothing is bliss, said someone, I don't know who, an old sage no doubt, and indeed it would seem that I have nothing to be unhappy about. In all modesty I can say I have at last reached that state of calm closed to me for those many years, I have my little house with its nearby river and the rolling green hills with the painterly sea beyond, so what more could I want when it couldn't be any better? To break the silence and disturb its peace? To speak? But what have I to say about myself? Nothing, less than nothing, I have no story to tell and when I did once try to tell you a story about myself you merely yawned and called it insipid and bogus. It was that, of course, but how else could it be when I do not even know myself and, I am first to admit it, when, though I have eyes to see, the magnificent abundance of the world's three dimensions seems to me no more than some hallucinatory, depthless and unpassable surface as untouchable and distant as your face even when I, effaced, look uncomprehendingly and uselessly at you? (You were an image for me first of all, come to think of it. Didn't I first see you in a photograph at that exhibition?) But rather than speak I can only remind myself to listen and try better to understand. I know how useless my entreaties would be, but to paraphrase the old sages again, as we regain the world only by first renouncing it, do we not also regain what we love only by renouncing all hope of possessing anything more than the image of this love, and is it not too preposterous to say that the infinite opening disclosed by the abyss separating us is also the locus of your infinite disclosure and revelation? Is this then what you mean when you say that you are nothing and is this your patient way of trying to enlighten me as to my own nothingness when, as I vainly attempt to master my thwarted cognizance of my situation with you, you counter my guileless, inquisitorial questions only with your cryptic, Zen koan replies?

But for the life of me, and because language knows more than I do and always gets the better of us, I barely yet understand myself what I am saying with such tortuous complexities and contradictions. The sun of her presence shines too brightly for my dumb incomprehension, but as I am both condemned to decipher the meaning, if any, of this encounter and condemned if I do not, I have no choice but to continue with my questioning. This unsought-for bliss multiplies itself endlessly but nothing will be gained from it, nothing brought to light, it will all go to waste and remain without issue if I cannot extract the alchemical quintessence of its precious knowledge, if I cannot stem its overflowing plenitude and distill its essence into a vessel small enough, like a vial of some heavenly perfume, to contain it. The untrammeled excess of its promise, its very levity would otherwise weigh too heavily, would leave me uninvited to its party and the universe would have passed me by. I would be a mere interloper, a spy, a mere toy of fate abandoned to the power of a slavish passion born of want if I did not retain that space in which I am able to reassemble myself, in which I can freely combine my hankering for infinity with my childlike love of surfaces, of flowers, trees and animals, of small, useless and futile things. Surely this time proud death will loose interest and overlook me. Who does he think he is, anyway, this angry, dissatisfied ignoramus of the first order with no precious secrets of his own to hide and who only repeats the monotonous platitude that everything passes?

She often recoils from me because of what she sees as my duplicity and timid hesitancy, but is it not out of fear of my obsessive desire to possess the object of my affections that I divide myself against her? Love always inspires fear, as it should, but am I such a country bumpkin that I could be so afraid of her charms? To set myself against her would only be dehumanizing, but I ask too much of her and fail her when I confound her embrace with the maternal, unconditional embrace of the world. Perhaps this failure is even inevitable and necessary, my gateway to her, perhaps the gap hollowed out by this failure will bring me, if not closer to her, at least close enough to touch the edge of that space she inhabits and where she simply is. I once believed that I would find the absolute, that 'precious diamond rendering me secure,' in some forgotten receptacle in the recesses of who knows what place, but no, it's with her, in this gaping space of failure, of love itself. Why look for dizzy raptures elsewhere? And if in my failure I am then left with nothing but this space, I may at least decorate it with arabesques, with labyrinthine castles of air, with a house, or better a cathedral, a temple, my own tawdry Taj Mahal in which I can live while I mark out its corners, hallways, rooms, windows and walls. A majestic structure will crystallize into being, a great, beautiful city of consciousness rising from beneath the waves like Venice, an impossible city populated by fabulous people and ghosts, its buildings with their own past as strangely and deeply significant as a dream. Aha, yes, yes! I have it now. I am an empty white page, yes, but this emptiness opened to me is infinitely more than what exists, the very idea of emptiness an empty one. Yes, of course! The absolute works with nothing, it uses what does not exist, its materials are what does not exist.

Her forerunner from years ago, yes, I remember now. Perhaps you and she are the same person, perhaps she is reincarnated in you, and she knew then that long after we had parted I would one day meet you and that you would become her future. The percussive waves, those nights of endless promise at the edge of the real. The old wooden house high on the slope overlooking the coastline of black rock. The maternal harbour with the passing, somehow significant lights of the ships at night going on their set ways, the horizon both promising and yet resisting transcendence, the confining limits of my own too-inward self, the plus beyond the enough, beyond the far limits of my meagre travels. The ambitious hopes we confided to each other when we said everything and nothing, the things we agreed on and the things she remonstrated me over. The time was new and gracious in its benevolence, it seemed to drown all hatred and bloodlust, to render them redundant and primitive. But we, even as two previously unrelated universes of discourse whose union would now solve the previously insoluble problem of everything and who dreamed of some intimated shared otherworld, each separately and silently knew and feared that one day she would go her own way to meet her undoubtedly full and eventful life and I, undoubtedly more impoverished and disappointed, to my own. No, already she was far beyond me in matters of the spirit, already, despite her youth, an initiate of the world's cryptic secrets, and I merely an ignorant peasant. What would ever bind us together in this world when we still had everything else to live by? I sensed in my delirious lucidity that I was at the point of discovering for myself the legendary Big Secret, but which, if I thought I knew then, I am certain that I do not know now or have at least almost forgotten. Above and beyond this time, we were participants not merely in a series of disjointed episodes and unnoticed events, in 'novels rarely read,' but in some epic, waking dream, lost in a world of ungraspable dimensions of which this time was only a partial and as yet unformed expression. It was perhaps the essence of space and time conjoined in the one crystallizing moment, and yet a time uncompleted and expecting completion in some impossible future, a magic carpet carrying us to some magical elsewhere, the time seeming to mark itself out, to find its own time, its own measure, to contain its own implied music with its own theme, subject, development, recapitulation and crowning, magnificent resolution. If the outside world laughed at me and called me deluded, I was yet prepared to risk being called as such. Beguiled, deluded, so be it. I would have been be a fool, anyway, not to love her. How more deluded I would have been to dismiss our meeting as a mere random product of chance? Hadn't I, at one moment, canceled chance and time's destructive effects, hadn't I found time's perfect, heavenly stasis?

But am I as alone and isolated from others as I in my less privileged moments incline to tell myself? No doubt such a sense of isolation is only one delusion amongst others, and we are never alone. From what I know about modern quantum physics, (I should read some books: make a note) I like to speculate that we have much in common with the quantum waves that define the colourful form and matter of the universe, that like them, all-embracing, inclusive, we are more than a single entity, more than one of many discrete quantum particles egotistically and blindly flying about their own business. It often seems that I do indeed have the sensation of being on a wave or even having become a wave or rather multiple waves of a great unknown ocean and that, even when separated by vast distances we, like two particles in quantum entanglement, are simultaneously conjoined across space in some unfathomable way. When I am with her am I not only one but simultaneously everyone?

A passing landscape of lightly browned hills punctuated by narrowly pointed trees seems permeated with a blithely buoyant spirit as I play the car radio for the five-hour drive. The soft music infuses the imposing plenitude of a landscape otherwise as unintelligible as the movements of a dancer when we can't hear the music she dances to. It makes it its own, choreographs it to its own patterns and rhythms, turning the lineaments of the mountains and hills into lines of phrases and sentences, bending its contours and curves to its own purposes. The rolling soft grey green hills with their gladdened, carefree cattle and sheep, the gentle ceramic blue sky opening onto the promise of the distant, impossible horizon and countries and cities beyond accessible by not much more than a day's flight. And yet, without her, the landscape, profuse as it is, is as incomplete and unaccomplished as I am, as though it too, like me, were still trying to understand and complete itself. Is there, after all, an afterlife, an unknown missing dimension beyond this? I seem to lack nothing and yet because the world seems incomplete without such a dimension, without the witty knot which would make sense of everything and hold it together. I understand those old clairvoyants now. They don't seem so mad now with their talk of an 'other side' simultaneous and coalescent with the present, of some mysterious dimension beyond the homely four dimensions of our own lives, and I swear I can hear the voices of my own distant ancestors from whom I left off when I was born, I can hear them speaking, singing, each one of them their own star in the night.

I like walking, I am a walker, and even as a child I was imagining wandering the great parks of the world, such as Boboli, Bushy Park, the Bois de Boulogne... I am walking in Paris, channeling the great walker Rousseau. I go to Greece and channel the great walker Byron, go to Austria and channel the great walkers Mahler, Mozart and Beethoven, go to German and channel the great walker Wagner, go to England and channel the great walkers Wordsworth, Keats and Shelley and go to Florence and channel the great walker Dante. All in the vague hope of meeting you. Even walking through autumn trees in the park I am thinking of you and of where you came from.

It's all a dream, as well all know. But for all their relentless, systemic activity and the fierce light they live under what are they running from or running towards, what, apart from crude survival, are they hoping to gain if not to escape from the world they want to create? It is tough out there nowadays, I know, and even in my childhood dreaming garden the gently curving path yields inevitability to the hostility of the roads and town beyond, but for me it is only in this garden with its eternal quiver of tulips, marigolds, dahlias and lilies, its murmuring trees, its sloping lawn, that it all begins and ends and where there is yet all the time in the world to do everything or nothing. If only then you were before me now. It was here, long ago, you see, that because, like all children, I was in love even without anything or anyone to love, I could thus never be robbed of what I loved. And even if the garden is haunted by unfinished, threadbare stories and histories, by the knowing ghosts of the dead and absent, if you were here now and decided to stay, because you are absence itself there would be no absence, nothing lost and no loss to grieve over, because you are the night there would be no night and all would be well again.

Fate

I can only hope that this malady of mine may yet contain its own cure. If I liked to see myself as one who takes an almost clinical pleasure in expunging illusions, both those of my own and of others, then it seems that now you, my invisible dark one, have pulled the rug from under me I am must admit that I am even less enlightened than I ever was, and if I like to see myself as calmly reasonable it now seems that such a view of myself has itself amounted to a delusion and I am well and truly caught in the web of the world's appearances. Even my books are no escape for me when, having once been led to believe that one could acquire clear and positive knowledge of everything from them, the only profit I have drawn is merely to have discovered my own ignorance when, being too interested in what happened and what was written in past centuries, I found myself ignorant of what was happening in the here and now. Having lost my calm reasoning, that gentle, reassuring physician to our ills, I find, to my own horror, that even if all else happily grows and comes into its own in its own way without me I do not know myself, I lack substance, I have lost any footing, I am out of time, unable to mark time, floating adrift.

It seems that it all began here in the eternal past of this photograph, the founding origin of my second and true life, and without which all this would not have been set in motion. I never set much store by reincarnation but in first seeing the picture I seem to know you already, it's the face of someone I know – I do not not know when and where. You are in the garden, facing the camera from the centre of the deep night, you are fixed in a moment which might as well be the measure of all time and space, and on either side of you, under the lamplight, wreaths and chains of flowers, pale, almost colourless, foolish and fearless, radiating into the blackness, the past converging on the clear skies at the summit of time, the fragrant light of a distant and boundless paradise diffusing old ghosts and demons, a unity of stars framing some unknown destiny or fate. I did not see you in person until some four weeks later and it took a few moments before I recognized you. This then is the background of our meeting. So it's true: the first time you see the beloved you sense you have seen her long before, it's true that love, like knowledge, is recollection. And where is the garden? It's the same one in my old town from childhood, the one I used to visit, the garden enclosed by dense trees and hedges, protected against the raucous traffic beyond. Once, having grown out of childhood, I wanted to escape from this familiar place and travel as far as possible but now, with a divine irony, time has brought me full circle to this place of original stillness to transfigure it with your presence.

What I assumed up till now as absolutely true and assured you have turned inside out and it seems that I, the stock character of the philosopher with his distrust of passions and enchantments, a Melvolio for whom ordinary people are idle shallow things, not of his element, have become my own laughing stock, a fool, a clown, with all my books, my toys, my ideas, my abstractions collapsing around me. At first I had thought you were merely naive, but it's I who am the naive one, it's I who don't know myself. If I am not to surrender myself to madness, what more then can I do but listen to myself as if I were another? Being human, after all, presupposes madness, but the way to fight such madness is to reflect on it with a sufficiently ironic detachment. That would be the only way to maintain any clarity, any transparency or agility or order. In my arrogance I told myself at the beginning of my encounter with you that it was going to be fun, a laugh, an entertainment or at most a kind of higher game, but now it has been escalating into a baroque, grandiose melodrama of the mind I have no power to block, from which I cannot extricate myself, and these driveling internal monologues of mine only serve to remind me how language is never innate and personal but always the language of the other, how I can only posit myself in relation to this other even if this other is more of a mystery than I can ever hope to fathom but without whom I am no more than an accident. How could I possibly break my silence and directly divulge to you in person such introspection when the very phenomena of my internal life are external and not mine, and not those of a first person singular 'I' but an impersonal 'it' through which they flow and against which I have little power? They pass through and in front and above me, whispering voices from my immortal soul, ghosts, word ghosts mocking me, singing their own song, until I am less substance than possibility. I like to think that you are my own creation, but isn't it the other way round? It's you who have summoned me from nowhere or some half-forgotten dream. Who was it, after all, who made me doubt the fixed substance of my own self, who has seeded in my soul such thoughts? Isn't it you who have set them in motion, encouraged them, spirited them into existence? But to speak them would embarrass you as much as it would embarrass me and I am thus resolved to keep my thoughts to myself and spare you the platitudes, as weak as watered-down table wine, that I might unleash on you. I wouldn't want to harm you. It would be better if I bore my evils alone, and it would be a bad recompense for your affections to lay any of them on you. It's not that words are too insubstantial but that they describe too much, they are too brutal for that of which I can't speak, they want more meaning than I can provide. And who, anyway. would have any interest in my vapid, tedious confessions? My inner life is nothing to write home about and, in all honesty, I care little for it. No one would want to hear about it, they would turn away, they wouldn't want to know me and it's all been said before, after all. My own problems are neither here nor there, everyone has them, I am not so unique, my past has been ordinary, I do not pretend to be anyone particularly special, I did not grow up in a tiny country town, I did not live on a farm, my parents were not brutally argumentative, I was not abused, I was not in a war, not a professional academic, a spy for MI6, I am not dying of cancer, I do not know anyone dying of cancer, I am not suffering from an overwhelming depression, my disposition is inherently, congenitally sunny, the sunlight does not impel me to flee from it into the dark, I do not argue with someone over the kitchen sink, the world beyond the paling fence does not pose a serious threat to me, I try to resist pandering to my own lowest instincts. When it comes down to it, for that matter, do I have any problems that I haven't invented for myself? I like, as they say, to rise to life's occasion. In vital matters such as this isn't it all a matter of form and grace over substance?

To you I am ridiculous when I display my anger, and at such times merely stare ahead indifferently and coldly into the distance, and even when you use kind words I suspect you are only humouring me.

I was accustomed to a retired, orderly existence, I told myself that I had it all infallibly under control and was the master of my own fate, or something like that, but now, with sublime irony, it is I who am being toyed with and as I have no choice in the matter, no doubt you will be the death of me. After that last debacle when I swore I would never love again and to that purpose erected for myself every prohibition against such involvements, when I decided once and for all to play the stoic and abhor all enchantment and magic, to distrust their hold over me, to frame them cynically as mere theatre, when I had thought it was all over, and had made a clean break of it, when I thought I was free from all cares and alarms, when I would be left in peace to apply myself to my long-postponed study of doubt and certainty, you have appeared from nowhere, undoing everything.

Some mundane, melodramatic, unworthy thoughts and inter-personal complications to follow: Am I then the victim of a joke, a trap, a plot, is she leading me down the garden path, or does she hold the Ariadne thread that would guide me out of this labyrinth? Isn't she aware of the kind of person I am? Why me, after all, and what does she see in me, of all people? She only replies that she has her reasons, but because words have grown false and she is loathe to reason with them, so she can't tell me. Perhaps she thinks I have money, perhaps she sleeps with everyone and I am only one amongst the others, perhaps is using me for some unfathomable end. What, indeed, is she then playing at and what is it, for that matter, that I am perhaps inadvertently playing at, despite myself? Do I want to see her again or not, what is to be done, how far am I prepared to go with this? I could tell her I don't want to see her, I could tell myself I don't want this interruption, and yet perversely, despite myself, I am as elated as if I had discovered the Holy Grail. And when I hadn't seen her for two weeks and thought it was hope-less and she had gone forever she came to the door that morning in person bringing with her the hope that my self-imposed sentence to solitary confinement would yet be reprieved and made unnecessary, that not all was as dissipated and entropic as I had come to believe in the earlier days of my disillusionment. It was precipitate of me to assume that it was all over once and for all and that I could ever predict the future. I say to myself 'Therefore it follows that..." But, of course, it doesn't necessarily follow at all. These 'therefores' are so many specious reasonings. The tragic, I should already know by now, is always apt to lurch into the comic. Perhaps there is hope af-ter all.

I would be deceiving myself if I thought that everything has not become superfluous without you, that the summer has not become winter, that the darkness of your absence, even if it only increases my thoughts of you, has not become intolerable. No, it's the very light of your presence I want. If I left home to travel somewhere else I would only spend my time thinking of you until, one day, even if I might forget you altogether, something would be taken from me, something precious missing and lost forever. More than a passing moment, you are necessary, you are necessity and fate itself, you hold my fate in your hands, and I think I may even well be in love with my fate. This fate is beautiful, it's beauty itself, it rests on the foundation of necessity. *Amor fati*: let that be my love henceforth! There's nothing I can do about it, and it will unfold with its own inevitable, internal logic in its own stately way as it blithely skirts catastrophe, tracing its own line into eternity beyond us. After all, it was under the guise of chance that fate in its indifference to our schemes and pursuits brought me to you. Who can deny this sublimely transcendental buffoonery that sees so clearly into our own intentions and arranges events for us for better or ill? To think, for example, that for years I was living in the same town as yours without knowing you! And now here you are, as I had always suspected, the Truth itself dressed in all your coloured, bejeweled finery, a truth more convincing than any fleshless abstraction or equation. But if the tonic chord of this encounter implies a resolving chord, and if the chord remains unresolved and everything ends on the broken circle of a question mark, what then? It's a mystery, but can I be satisfied with a mystery? The problem presents itself and as such calls for a symmetry, an end to my beginning. But whatever, let everything expand endlessly into the ether of the universal, come what may. Who am I to question it? Take this chance. How often in the past have I lost because I hesitated? It was blind of me to resist such moments as inconsequential accidents, as passing temptations. I would also regret a life I could have led but did not, with its pages missing or empty. The world, someone said, is full of beautiful things but less so of beautiful moments, and beauty unveils itself to us only once. Yes, sometimes, when all is mysteriously still, the world that was once immobile begins to resuscitate, nature defrosts, re-energizes, everything begins to advance in a headlong dance. I am beginning to see the inexplicable clarity and aptness of things, there are moments of *claritas* and *veritas*, moments when I would say Yes to the eternal return of all things and for whose sake I would live this life all over again.

You are by the sequined sea, at Thorne Bay, Takapuna. Further inland the warring factions, the ceaseless effort, the dynamic impatience, the impatient trafficking, but here, against the effortlessly coherent movements of sea and sky, waves arriving rhythmically in their own time and no one else's, I can talk to you and gather my own coherence. All is in its place and somehow I know it will end as it has begun on this little cove with its curve of beach and scattering of black rocks, the sea populated with its ancient dreams and mythologies, the horizon the sublime gateway to knowledge and possibility.

I had become only an experiment in search of knowledge, a question, a line of inquiry, I was both the question and the answer, I was the enigma I must solve, the key I must unlock.

I was born to meet you, but when others speak of you they speak a language I don't understand and it's of someone else I don't recognize, someone I have never met. What do you see in her? they ask. You a fantasist, an idle day-dreamer merely seeking distraction. Have you lost your marbles? It's dangerous to be so excessively attached to one person, let it all go, it's not the end of the world if you don't see her again, there are plenty of others. And I am almost tempted to concede that, yes, they are right, it's impossible, it's ridiculous, I am too old for you, it's all a matter of my shambolic hormones and you are a mere fabulation of my own vanity. What am I thinking? But what do they know, after all? They tell me

I am being reckless but this is not merely a matter of chance, you are not merely one amongst the many and my encounter with you is not a random event but seems somehow predestined. How could I not believe that you have somehow been sent by some benevolent, miraculous power, that you are that apparition from another realm I imagine you to be, even if you do not know it yourself, and how could I feign Buddhist indifference and non-attachment to you when you yourself are my unknowable, untouchable, distant Absolute?

Is it any wonder you accuse me of duplicity when I try to excuse my hesitation and evasion? You suspect that I only see past you, that I am seeking a transcendent ideal through and beyond you and therefore, in my own way, using and abusing you and that I will only abandon you when I have found this ideal. And yet if you were only the visible form of this ideal to me and my thoughts were indeed searching for something beyond you, I would be contemptible. I know the type too well: when, triumphant and full of relief, having found his way to a glimpse of heaven by way of his friend, he counts his lucky stars and leaves her, or she conveniently dies and because she is dead he can claim anything anything he likes about himself and his intentions towards her, and in his own eyes he is redeemed, all sins forgiven because of it.

If I maintain ironic detachment from myself it is not that I would also maintain such detachment from you. I am not the arrogant ironist who himself becomes the shadow of the lifeless world he despises and would forgo and I only maintain enough distance from myself to save myself from the ignominy of being wholly unconscious of my own behaviour or inward turmoil. I am dangerously too close to myself as it is, I know how easily I deceive myself in matters closely concerning me, but I have, I would hope, at least come to sufficient accommodation with the paradoxical duality of what it is to be human, the self-contradiction, for example, of seeming in my own eyes at once both myself and someone else, both innocent and guilty, both false and true. I am both of this world and not of it, and if we are primordially fallen creatures, which I doubt, such a fall posits the standard by which it defines itself and I, not so innocent as to be unaware of my fall from grace, am not incognizant of that state in which I was not fallen, untouched, above the fray, and unentangled in the world's duplicity. I have my own notions of such a state.

Who do I consult to find my proper place in the rumblings of this world's affairs, what is my vocation in this world into which I was thrown at birth with no choice in the matter? It's business as usual, everyone out to make a buck and good luck to them, but of what use, for what profit are these cold strivings for contained efficiency if you are unaware that any life by definition is a permanent overflow, an overwhelming, squandering excess?

More mundane, melodramatic, complicating events with often venomous, hypocritical and unreliable self-justifications: Perhaps A is jealous of me and merely wants me out of the way. Now that she is seeing him perhaps I will never see her again but, after all, why shouldn't she see someone else? Having as yet made no declaration of my intent accusations of infidelity don't come into it, but I wonder if I want to take on the responsibility that such a declaration would impose on me. If we were to live together, what then? She would doubtless quickly tire of my innate melancholy and find me out.

Who is this nemesis of mine? He has money, he is conventionally successful, with a house, two cars and so on, but perhaps he is not so clever as he would like to think. What can she possibly see in someone for who reduces all phenomena to physics and formulae, for whom consciousness is only a biochemical byproduct and who so shamelessly abuses truth in the service of the false? Who is he, this pragmatic technocrat with no sense of the metaphorical or the lyrical, what are his motives, if any; who is he, this Iago of mine with his textbook jokes passing for humour, his platitudinous remarks intended as a display of depth? Has he no shame before that virtue and 'beauty as weak and powerless as a flower' which he knows, to his own rage, he is yet powerless to demean and destroy? Who does he think he is and what does she see in him, she of all people, and how on earth was he able to interest her in him in the first place? I am jealous, but my jealousy is beneath me, it's vulgar even if I have justificatory cause for it, but yes, I admit, I am jealous.

What was I thinking? What was I jealous about? Did I need jealousy? He has gone, he has to leave town to attend to his affairs somewhere and it would seem any relations, if there were any relations between them, are over.

I would save much wasted time and energy if the future were not the mere hypothesis it is but somehow foreseen and resolved and written on some stone tablet in the distant past. What a thing that would be! I would only have to read it, decipher it and all would be explained and set before us. Perhaps one day I will become become estranged from you and when we meet again nearly fail to recognize one another. Or perhaps not. Who knows?

The Glass Cage

I am unable to submit to the embrace of this gentle scene. This seaside cove with its happy serenity pure of all perplexity and iniquity, its pale, porcelain sky, its sea flat as a sheet of glass awash with shifting colours varying between roseate and Pacific turquoise, does not mirror any serenity of my own but only teases my restlessness. The butterflies bounce about in the joyous air and yet, unlike them, I have yet to emerge from my own chrysalis of a self to fly upwards, metamorphosed, into a second life. If the world is billions of years old and yet, brimming with sprightly hope and expectation, it yet seems younger than me and it is only I who am old because not yet truly born.

In this place where everything happens that can happen and everything lives and acts and minds its own business, where, as I surely must, do I fit into all this? Overwhelmed as I am by this abundance I would, at the very least, like to somehow contain in the simplest possible way this swarming magnitude in capsular, ideal form, to reduce this ocean of infinitude to a single, crystalline drop small enough to view and contemplate.

Perhaps, after all, everything begins and ends here at this seaside cove opening out to the ocean beyond, and what more apt place is there than the ocean to inspire thoughts about infinity, to dream, to fabricate things from nothing, to weave invisible patterns and images in the sky, to meditate and speculate?

I should listen to myself, to this mysteriously transparent yet apparently intractable self I call my own.

But what is this transparent 'I', this self with which I am at once so intimate and from which I am so far removed, what is the absolute, primary foundation of this transcendental 'I' unbounded by any categories or finite determination? For too long now I have felt imprisoned within this self of mine as if by an invisible glass cage, apparently free to do anything and yet because of this infinite freedom infinitely unfree, but perhaps this cage is of my own making, perhaps what I take to be my freedom is my own glass cage and I don't know it.

As this is a friendly kind of place, A, a vivacious woman, still youthful in her fifties, approached me yesterday on the beach and casually introduced herself. I have noticed her on the beach several times and as we speak it soon emerged that she knows about me, most likely, I imagine, from someone in town. She asked me to visit her in her house situated a hundred yards or so down the coast, so here I am. She makes tea, shows me the rooms with their off-white walls, Edwardian wicker chairs, decorative shells, carefully placed maritime paintings and prints. From the framed photographs of her it appears that in perhaps happier times she was popular in all the social circles, a star in her own right. But while she voices her own thoughts and preoccupations why does she not address me directly? She could almost be using me as an audience or a mirror to practice a performance of some kind.

The visit does not end so amicably when she invites me back the following day and I, lying, tell her that because I have an urgent matter in town to attend to I won't, unfortunately, be able to come. Another time, perhaps.

Today, as I wander again down the beach, I can see a girl, or rather a young woman of perhaps nineteen years who, seeing me glance at her, momentarily returns my glance as we pass by, and that she responds at all, however minutely, only goes to remind me of how far out of the loop and how invisible to myself I have become. I should get out more, I should converse, be more sociable, I should speak freely and risk making a fool of myself like everyone else.

For a few days now I have seen her accompanied by what appear to be two of her girlfriends, or perhaps sisters. Recently the threesome have almost become a fixture of the scenery and appear regularly every day. Yes, it appears they are sisters: like sisters they remonstrate and argue amongst themselves.

I see A and what J strolling together on the beach. I didn't know that A was J's mother. I wouldn't have noticed the resemblance.

Later in the day on the beach I see J by herself. I am curious. I want to see her again, to speak to her, but how will I approach her? I would give anything to say something to her, no matter how trivial. What shall I do? 'How to speak to the angels,' indeed. Behave casually, inconsequentially? What is my cue? I don't want to scare her away. Sometimes I can hear her voice, neither harsh nor shrill. Let what happen happen, there is plenty of time, she doesn't appear to be going anywhere fast.

The opportunity has duly arisen. Fate or destiny or whatever you call it has its way when J appears at the door one day telling me her mother has invited me to her house. So, now for the narrative, the background plot, the complicated family drama, which, on the surface, has little to do with anything I have ever taken interest in before and little to do with my philosophical investigations. I ask J in. At last we are talking. "I didn't know you were A's daughter. Are you living here or on holiday?" I say. Too much, too much too soon. Stop. Why didn't A come herself? I ask myself. I sense that somehow A has not sent her as an emissary on her own behalf but rather for some other, perhaps more secretive reason, perhaps with designs on me, perhaps to acquaint me and J with each other. But why me when I have all the appearance, some would say, of a seducer? Or is A using J to somehow take her revenge on me for refusing her? Is she one of those women who train their daughters to break men's hearts to avenge her own broken heart?

Perhaps I should tell J more about myself, I should write to her, but then again I might embarrass myself, I might embarrass her and resort to the kind of cold abstractions and speculations which are my want. If I know I have something of the cold aesthete and callous libertine in me, I am yet on guard against this and I should try to convey the correct impression: neither too virtuous nor too flirtatious. Is she unknowing of her effect on me? In some sense yes, and I suspect she knows more than she tells, being, I suspect, one of those ancient souls who already seem to know everything without having read or traveled widely. She says that if her two sisters are practical and successful in their own way, she was always considered a dreamer, never quite of this world, and perhaps even mad. Taking a genuine and innocent interest in my books on ancient art, she indicates details in some of the pictures that I had not noticed and seems to understand the meanings, the symbols and mythology behind them without, it would appear, any knowledge of history or art.

She is one of those people who seems to belong to both West and East, to all countries, to all races, all times. Can I tell her, without embarrassment, that she is my charming enigma, the pathway to my own soul, my very own muse?

J tells me after we have known each other two weeks that I am not what she expected. "And what did you expect?" I reply. "Someone disreputable," she says. "I've heard stories about you. Something almost defiant in me persuaded me to come to you, and if my mother thought you were disreputable, well, you can imagine this only made you all the more interesting and curious for me." "Perhaps you are right, I counter. "I don't have the highest of reputations. So what do you think of me now? What is it, who do you see?" "I hardly know you," she replies. "How can I describe you? Who are you, anyway? Tell me about yourself." "Must I tell you about myself? How can I answer that?" I reply. "Why so secretive?"

she asks. "Do you need to know everything? I have done nothing criminally suspect, I have no shady past, if that's what you mean," I counter again. "Don't talk nonsense. That isn't what I mean," she says, and to put the matter to rest and stop myself going around in circles perhaps I should confess that I, well, that I love her, but I sense she already knows and understands this, even if I don't. "What are you writing in your notebooks? Can I read them? Are they about me?" I ask. "About everything, and yes, you are there, but they are merely crude scribbles, jottings of no consequence, a loose and disparate connection of notes which it would embarrass me to show to anyone in their present form. It would destroy everything. Sometimes too much can be said, and said wrongly." Sometimes too much is indeed said and especially, for that matter, in our private confessions to ourselves which too often amount to confused fictions or justifications for our past and present actions.

But if she is being honest with me is she also being honest with herself? What is she telling herself about me and does she think I am some kind of monster, a Caliban? But no, I don't think so, and I am ashamed of myself for such unworthy suspicions. We speak to each other, we are candid, she allows me to say everything, doesn't she? She is not easily embarrassed, she wasn't born last week, she is no wide-eyed innocent and, to the contrary, even at her age seems like one of those old but eternally youthful souls who, like Leonardo's Lisa, we imagine already knows everything worth knowing.

J's sisters want to visit us because they hadn't seen her for a while, they were missing her and also wanted to meet me. I said that of course they could visit to put the matter to rest and see that I was not the demon they suspected. When they duly arrived they were friendly enough, critically, sometimes condescendingly surveying the house like an exacting landlady, but finally they told me I was fortunate to be living in such a nice house and grounds, implying, it seemed to me, that I was hardly worthy enough for such grandeur and had somehow come into possession of it by accident or some otherwise devious means. They are visibly annoyed when they ask J if she was coming home and she replies that no, she would be staying here with me. Are they to be the ugly sisters of this Cinderella drama?

J's sisters are wielding the knife again, trying to turn her against me. They too had heard stories. What stories? That I had had 'a past' and was holding something back, but if I am holding something back I am unconscious of what it could be. "Why am I standoffish?" J asked. "If they suggested I find out more about you, do some research, make inquires, it is only because they care for me," she said, disingenuously, I thought. I doubted it. I said "Do they think I am a well-known criminal in hiding? I'm sure they could always dig up some dirt on me if they wanted." "But whatever the case, I like being here with you, I'm happy. I'm afraid you would leave me if I asked any more questions. What can I say, why must I explain everything? Let's not raise the subject again," she replies.

Today, being at their critical and spiteful best, it is barely possible to have a conversation with the sisters. They seem to harbour resentment against everything and everyone, no doubt, I would surmise, out of some past trauma after which they seem either to have either forsworn love, or more likely, having never known it, and I suspect the latter. They live pragmatically from day to day, continuously pressed for time carrying out their errands or working for their commerce exams, there is endless work to be done but I fear that it will never be done and they will spend all their lives complaining of lack of time to do it. Already having lost any vestige of youthful innocence they have not yet regained that vital, second, wiser innocence borne only of experience, and afraid of the natural spiritedness of things, of the unknown, of what cannot easily be explained or formulated, they have turned cynical with a vengeance. To them J is a failure, a loser, an old-fashioned Romantic who won't face reality, whatever that is. But as always and as I was always warned when young, I shouldn't judge too hastily and perhaps somehow these sisters have a role to play in all this, perhaps they have at least had the effect of prompting me to question my own motivations. But why the sisters' unhealthy loyalty to their mother, why do they persistently so act on A's behalf? No doubt they are jealous of J's independence and seem desperate to unmask me to J as the monster they believe I am, even though they can surely have little knowledge of my background. But enough of all this cheap, melodramatic psychology. I am not living in a fool's paradise, there is always something or someone hissing venom somewhere away in the background, and they could be right, I am nearly twice her age and too old old for her, and perhaps if they see me as unsuitable, they have every right to question me, a complete stranger, no prince looking for his Cinderella and possibly a madman.

Someone who knows the family tells me that A was once a successful businesswoman in public relations, but if she was the mistress of order in her professional life she was also the servant of her own unconstrained emotions combined with a callousness often beyond any moral considerations, someone, I imagine, who would swallow men whole and anyone else who would get in her way. This would explain a lot when I notice men admiring J from a distance almost as if one might notice with a start a visiting goddess passing by in some mundane street and were too intimidated to approach, as A, I am sure, was once such a goddess and sees J, so different from her in so many other ways, usurping what was once her own unassailable position amongst such immortals. Is this why A, out of jealousy and spite, has tried to demote J from her place in the social firmament and bring her down a few steps for having descended from such heights to fall in with a mere mortal such as myself?

When J told me today that A is ill and needs her to look after her, I had to ask: What about her sisters? Can't they help? But as I should have known A is not so ill as she claimed, that she's playacting and I surmise it's merely another way of keeping J her prisoner. But why is it that A seems so in conflict with herself when, on the one hand, she would marry J off to anyone who would have her and yet, on the other, she would keep her at home all day at her own bidding for fear of loosing her whenever someone appears.

Today I visited J, but only A is at home. For some unknown reason A is pleased to see me, perhaps because mistakenly she believes that I have come to see her and her only and am only using J as a pretext. You are not really interested in J, are you? she asked impatiently. J is silly, spoilt, vain, she says, she lives off her looks, she does not know herself and will need to learn some unhappiness and humility before she can come into herself. J told me that she loves you. Love? Love, I ask you. What does J know of love? Before I left I asked again about J and where she was. At first she displayed a flash of annoyance and yet, coming full circle again, unexpectedly turned more conciliatory. "J will be back tomorrow and I will tell her you came," she says. Why the change in attitude then? Perhaps in her devious way she sees me as the unhappiness she would like to inflict on J, that I am the convenient weapon and my role would be to merely toy with her affections and one day cast her aside.

I have not seen J for a few days now and already missing her I am beginning to fixate on her, but I must wait things out and take care not to make a hasty move. Let things work themselves out for themselves.

J is doing the housework, obsessively exaggerating each wipe of the kitchen surface and I am beginning to worry for her. Too often A and the sisters make her stay at home and clean the house like the Cinderella they take her for. "Why are you working like a slave?" I ask. "I like to make order out of things," she replies. "It's a way of staying ahead of myself." I understand her as this is exactly what I am doing in another sense: sorting, collating, ordering, cutting and pasting my own thoughts and notes. She doesn't exactly know which way to turn, she continues, when it seems that her entire life stands before her like an empty white page. "How do people live with so little and yet so much?" she says. Having never traveled, this muchness for her seems far beyond the horizon, fabled yet not seen with her own eyes, and if she is to live with herself and dissipate the lawless dreams and fantasies flowing about in her own mind she thinks she must taste some of this grand muchness for herself. She wants to sort herself out. Yes, she thinks she will travel the world, visit the lost homes of her ancestors, visit her Venetian relatives, the di Zanchis, who always wanted to see her. Venetian? She revealed to me that, unlike her sisters, or rather stepsisters, she was adopted and had known this since she was little. She had traced the relatives, she had written to some of them. This journey might at least take her some way out of her confusion, and yes, I agree, it would be a way of being able to look down on or outside of herself, a way to help her see the world as the small globe it is rather than the overwhelming, impossible mass of infinity it might seem to her now, and by gaining such an overview she may learn how better to choose amongst the many possibilities available to her. She also wants to learn from the past, from ancient history, from that history which she believes, despite one's own allotted span of life, is also the history and summary of ourselves. She believes the world today in its modernity is not all that it cracks itself up to be, that it lacks memory, indeed often forswears memory, and despite its constant penchant for change, it merely repeats itself maniacally.

A, to whom J has already told her all her new plans, swept in today and berated J with the familiar parental commonplaces: "You want to leave, after all I have done for you? You have everything here but you refuse it all?" Even her sisters join the fray and accuse J of reckless selfishness: "You will come to no good," and so on.

But today in another surprising or rather not so surprising about-face her mother gave her blessing to her travels and told her she would pay for the trip, with all accommodation included. I suspect this is A's way of removing J altogether from my sight, and the sisters will no doubt also take perverse delight in my loss.

Henceforth there can be no safe haven for me. Shall I confess my feelings for her now? But she might read this as a silly infatuation, a pleasurable pretense and indulgence on my part, and if the artless, hesitating clumsiness with which I already speak to her is anything to go by I am afraid of saying it wrongly. I can think anything I like but when it comes to saying what I think then how little I am able to convey, especially since I dislike the sound of my own voice. If only poetry were ready at hand. I have become a stranger to myself, and not knowing what to say I find myself borrowing other people's lines and playing the role of an actor playing the part of someone who loves, even if that someone is only myself, and I am obliged to adopt the part of every lover and mouth every cliché in every play or novel ever written. Will I be adequate to this new self of mine? If I disclose my affections for her, assuming they are genuine, what will happen, what will it alter, how might this disturb the order of things? Perhaps she isn't interested in me. Jealousy: yes, I admit it, I am jealous of this world in which she belongs and on whom it shines, everyone celebrates her, but at least I should admit that my jealousy is enough to demonstrate to myself that I don't want to loose her and that everything depends on her presence. But I am loathe to indulge this jealousy of mine and prefer at the very least to feign a lack of it because, for that matter, I have no urge, no egoistic mania to possess anyone or anything and win at all costs. It is a singular individual, it is she I am pursuing and no one else, it is not as though there were others I might readily exchange her for at the slightest whim, it is not as though mine were no more than a passing aesthetic involvement from which I could readily detach myself and allow to pass by with a kind of cinematic passivity. No, I am moving now into what they call the ethical dimension and I ought not waver, I will decide for good or ill, and I certainly can't go on like this. Next time I will confess, I will tell her that I do not want to toy with her affections and would like to somehow formalize our relations.

Fearing for things to come, seeing signs and portents and show-ing me things I wouldn't normally see beyond the grey membrane that normally blurs and discolours my own view of the world, you know more than I do, you see further, you see around the corner of time. You, the supernatural fracture in the order of things, my way out of my glass cage, the confounder of my endless argument with myself, have you come from some place in another life prior to my own to become my guide through the underworld and beyond, my Beatrice, my pathway to my own joyful, smiling Absolute?

Sometimes when I volunteer to confess my doubts and turmoils she, like Beatrice to Dante, questions my cognitive capacity and, looking piteously on me as a mother on a child who never learns and will be the bane of mankind, patiently tries to explain to me the manifest order and structure of the world in which I only see chaos. All our aspirations and desires, she intimates in so many words, are providential rather than obstructive and all designed to lead us to that ground of being I am always harping on about.

Today I wandered into my study to find J reading my notebooks and diary. I was angry, of course, and who wouldn't be when, after all, I value such privacy and resent any invasion of it as much as anyone else? Startled, and startled again at my aggressive, impul-sive reaction, my "Don't look at that!" or some such exclamation, she merely countered indifferently that they were open on the table, available for anyone to browse and for that matter might well have been published for the whole world to see. Yes, she's right, but perhaps, even unconsciously, I had wanted her to see them.

I can only surmise that her sisters, enraged by the popularity and admiration she enjoys everywhere, have encouraged her constant curiosity and questioning in their efforts to damage me. It is they who must be behind all this, surely. All this espionage explains everything. When I try to make some excuses for my scrawls as mere throwaway lines of no importance she only asks me why I didn't tell her directly what I had written, and neither embarrassed nor angry tells me how my words simply revealed more about myself than about her and, moreover, that she was even moved by how the tender thoughts I displayed on paper were at such contradictory variance with the hardness of my behaviour. But everything is irrevocably changed now for me and having shone this harsh lamp on that darkness of soul and ugly desperation I was trying to hide from her she has ruined everything and broken the magic spell. To this she replies that her discovery only dispels her silly, girlish suspicions now she realizes what her sisters were up to and that what her sisters told her about me was spiteful and ignorant nonsense. "And why care so much about what I think about you, after all?" she continues. "Those unguarded thoughts you have been unafraid even to tell yourself show you as you are and not the intimidating and arrogant egoist I often accuse you of being. I was blind, I had blind faith in you from the beginning, you were only a face in the dark, but now I know you, I can see you, I understand, I have seen you as if for the first time. You don't think, do you, that I can so naïve, that I could be so easily embarrassed by such confessions? I was expecting ridicule, unkind things, but you have no hard words for me in these pages and all you do is harmlessly expose your own doubts and questions." I reply melodramatically that I am embarrassed by them now that she has exposed me to the light of day can see me now for the egomaniacal monster I must seem. They were intended as my own vault of secrets, my refuge. Monster? She says. "I can at least admire your honesty with yourself." But I know it is already too late, our period of ignorant, simple bliss is over and already I am falling away, taking fright, taking flight, retreating from so much that is known but which I don't want to know. When she leaves the house, upset, I preciously castigate myself once again: being the most naïve of romantics, forever pitting myself both against myself and the world, how rarely, to my own misfortune, do the world of ideas, art and imagination versus the prosaic matters of the everyday coincide for me.

A few days later, before I was about to tell her that I was leaving the area for a few days, she told me that she had indeed decided to travel. Where to? To Europe. She wanted to see the world, she had decided. How long would she be away? Six months, perhaps, but she didn't know. So much for that then, and who can blame her? What more can I do and say? After all, she is young and ought to travel.

A month later, with everything ready, she has left the country, saying goodbye with only a tear or two at the airport, leaving me to my black abyss of loss, brutally exposed to the folly of my own solipsism and with only my bedraggled thoughts for company:

When I say 'I' and 'You,' about whom and to whom am I speaking? Who is it, who am I who walks along this beach and the stretch of rocky coastline, who is it who is thinks, dreams and remembers, who is it beset by memories and images from the past: places, events, historical events, cultural history, hundreds or thousands of years of writing, music, of earlier ways of seeing the world, the ancient mysteries, Egypt, Greece and so on. But what is still left undone and unsaid, and what is now to be done?

Words hopelessly attempting expression of the absolute whose light appears fleetingly only to return to the darkness it has illuminated.

Beauty, at once distant yet near, that morning gate through which we must pass to enter the land of knowledge, that veiled, strange perfection both indifferent yet strangely comforting and understanding, only wants to draw me to itself and into its bright mystery and secrets without which everything would fall down.

Impossibly, I imagine myself on a mountain overlooking everything as I bless the wound that led to my cure. The sun shines on everything, I have found the alchemical rebus, the whole contained in the single Idea, the Philosopher's Stone, the totality that contains all contraries and excludes nothing. I can imagine audaciously asking myself one day at some impossibly distant time: what to do now that I have everything, when what I lost I have found and it would seem I can now do anything? It would almost seem that I have come full circle and reached a completion of sorts, the big important questions answered, that I survey in triumphant gratitude the realms of my own recovered, redeemed past and what was once pointless and meaningless now seems, retrospectively, as plotted as any old Greek drama, a series of clever devices to ferry me to this very moment where the sun illuminates everything with its glory and brings into clear relief all that was secretive and obtuse. The world will go on without me, but what do I care? That I have kissed the hem of the goddess and drunk life's cup is enough.

A vision of fields and blithely confident red and violet flowers, a stream running nowhere, a giggling waterfall, all this as pretty as a picture, yes, a place beyond the limits of the explicable, an expectation, with more meaning than the vision could alone provide.

Six in the morning. The room with the ebony and ormolu death clock. Can I turn the clock back or is time irreversible? The day's objects come into focus and regain their reassuring solidity as I awake from dreams of phantom characters and scenes merging with half-conscious and disconnected memories from the distant past, memories of books read, thoughts of books unread and perhaps never to be read, memories of those chance moments and small objects that were sometimes also mysterious connecting pathways to something or someone else, to something other.

Philosophers, often somewhat puritan, are unwilling to fall for the seductions of the natural world and yet seem easily seduced enough by abstractions, by ideas and ideals. Sometimes they cling to them for dear life, like fragments of wood floating on the sea after a shipwreck.

Perhaps I am my own worst obstacle, my own worst enemy, and yet again perhaps I want obstacles and enemies, perhaps they are necessary, perhaps they are my own secret friends, my helpers and guides, perhaps limits open the space for the transcendent.

Men will piss on anything sacred to make a buck out of it. 'A thing of beauty is a joy for ever,' as well as a nice fat commodity for sale.

It is now two years since she left and, apart from a few scattered messages to her mother to assure her of her own safety, and along with two postcards to me, we have not heard from her.

But what have you left me with in your absence but the un-exposed negative picture of all those elements which comprise a whole, a universe?

Can I speak such private, disjointed thoughts to you in person? What would I say to you that I would normally say only to myself in secret? I would not say what I meant to say. What is not said is said and what is said is not said, and conscious of this I can't help but play the disingenuous ironist as soon as I open my mouth. With all that was familiar and known exploded into fragments, I still don't know anything more than I did when I was twenty.

But your absence is the necessary space in which to speak with myself. Yes, death or absence are convenient for such meditations, the private breeding ground for all kinds of repulsive self-justifica-tions, but to be closer to someone you must sometimes place yourself at a distance; you part from someone only so you can see that other again later as if for the first time. I could say all this to you, but how silly it would seem and, anyway, no words would come, or if they did I could not stop myself mangling them the moment they came out of my mouth. Love, like joy, has no language of its own and the old clichés would undermine me if I tried to speak. Only in music can you say anything you like and know that no one will be hurt because no one need know anything about its subject, and yet, unable to sing to save myself, I cannot sing those words too silly to be spoken.

Last night at the nearby restaurant a band struck up, but its music was unsettling to me. Its colourful, laughing exuberance, at reckless variance to the unworldly disorder of my own thoughts and emotions, was mocking the solemn earnestness of my present yearnings and I wanted a more sublime kind of music redolent of Olympian transcendence to match hem. But what else was this music really telling me other than to clean this idealistic nonsense out of my system, to get over myself, to snatch the moment? It was not the world which is broken and irredeemable, it is saying, but yourself.

I am the wound I want to heal, but what is the cure of this wound? This music is not going to provide it. It is a distraction, a mere dressing, a palliative rather than cure.

Did I know paradise before my fall or did the very idea of paradise arise only after I fell and it was only this state of brokenness that suggested that famed state of original, unbroken unity, that perfect world in which what you say is always understood, when words mean what they say and words and things are never at odds with one another?

Is everything until now haphazard, meaningless, demeaned and luckless or am I somehow being tested as in some German Bildungsroman? Or if there is meaning, there are only various meanings and counter-meanings colliding in waves, in eddies constantly changing, colliding or passing each other by. But do I even expect or even want the resolution of a meaning, if resolution there must be? Of course I do.

You open me out to the void without return. What have I to return to, anyway?

To puncture this child's balloon of an illusion, if illusion it is, in the name of some chimerical abstract truth or bodiless certainty, would also be to fall into a deeper illusion, would be as vulgar as to ridicule a stage setting or painting in the name of an absolute verisimilitude. It would be an easy but cheap thing to do at the behest of a reality of which I, anyway, know little and to whose claims for itself I am often loathe to lend much credence. But am I truly deceived? No, the sisters have been planting the seeds of such doubt and suspicion in me, I'm sure. Time itself is the detective who will disclose any truth it may have to tell, the secret will be out and the veil lifted, and when the veil of this dreamlike illusion parts, tearing the flimsy gossamer fabric of reality to shreds, what will it reveal? You, I have no doubt, only you standing before me.

Joy: Those moments of supreme, rapturous consciousness when you perceive the world with perfect clarity and it overflows into play, music and poetry. No dead facts or certainty can contradict it and they dissolve into its oceans, swallowed up like ice. With it you see vast distances and comprehend everything as if you were to look back from an indecipherable detail of a painting to reveal its place in a much vaster painting, each figure and detail a contributor to the overarching meaning and composition. Or it might be as if a motion picture were reversed and you viewed the shattered components of a world once rent asunder now regathering themselves into their former, pristine order.

Tragic or comic? From the perspective of eternity the tragic always veers towards the comic.

You know more than I like to think it you do, you know more than unhappiness knows because you are deeper, far deeper than unhappiness.

Impossibly, I like to imagine myself one day not as an everyday 'I' but a newly evolved kind of 'I' expanded and filled to the over-flowing with a Dionysian joy consequent on some quasi-religious ecstasy subject to no external imperative or law.

You have found me out at last. I had thought that you would re-veal me for the beast you perhaps suspected I was but instead, to my horror, you have found the God in me, even if I am afraid to con-front such a God and, unprepared as I am, afraid this God would destroy me. Not to be obliterated by such a power and retain some dignity demands a degree of aesthetic remove, an opposing Apol-lonian grace and lightness of touch to hold it in balance. Make a note of this.

What did I discover when you found me out? Number One: That I am not the 'I' that I thought I was, not the lost, primordial, parochial, unified self I had lost and mistakenly hoped that one day I might re-find. Number Two: That I am divided and was divided at the very source, that the origin is the two and not, as commonly believed, the one. Number three: It is this very division that enables me to converse with myself and stage my world. Number four: It's the same primordial division that separated the sky and earth in the old myths and allowed the Gods and Goddesses to procreate, the same division that makes everything possible.

Truth is not indivisible and could not recognize itself as truth if it were. It could not speak.

At any moment of loss I refuse happiness on the grounds that I can learn more from this unhappiness but, of course, the only use for unhappiness is to suggest a way out of it and reach happiness again.

Today A came to the door. I have not seen her so changed. She has heard nothing from P and is worried something has happened. Has she died, has she been stricken ill, did she fall permanently in with someone else? We don't know. She confesses that only now does she realize that her cruelty towards her was the effect of her own jealousy and assures me that my continued demonstration of devotion to J has so caused her to revise her opinions of me that she no longer sees me as the duplicitous libertine she once took me for. She knows I want now to take my place in the world with my feet firmly on the ground and that I won't be going anywhere.

My dream last night, beautiful and terrifying all at once: deep within a cave I come across a magic casket in which I hope to discover at last the answer to the Big Mystery but when I open the casket there is nothing there, nothing but darkness, but of course, I realize in a flash, this nothing is everything, my everything, and only then do I awake.

I am beginning to understand now, I am beginning to understand everything.

One day A tells me that she has heard from J that she will be coming home soon, and, indeed, seven days later there is a knock on the door. Who is it? Is it her or someone else?

Venice

Where am I now, what am I doing here and what time is it? Is it time to sleep or awake? It should be the morning but it feels like the evening. What am I doing in this looking-glass world with all of time and space out of joint, why out of all possible places and circumstances am I here where only a day ago I was not? And who, anyway, is this 'I' to which I was born, this 'I' sometimes burning in its own light, sometimes lost in darkness, this 'I' amongst all the other 'I's' and beings in the world? Perhaps I have taken leave of my senses. Why am I not at home doing the things I should be doing and what business have I here anyway? Perhaps I am on holiday but why do I even need a holiday? Do I have enough money for a holiday? Yes, of course I do, I have enough. But how long will it last? Only yesterday I was at home on the other side of the world 18,000 kilometres away, but I was transported somewhere else overnight and must now quickly accommodate my new surroundings in my consciousness. At least I am beginning to establish that I am not at home in my room with its familiar furniture, with the bay window overlooking the garden and trees and the light rumble of traffic beyond the hedges, but in the middle of nowhere, left only with myself with no one I know and none of my own books at hand. No books, but perhaps, anyway, I read too many, and I came here to escape from them. Books aren't everything, you can't get everything out of a book, the world will go on existing without me whether I like it or not, even if I once stupidly thought that if it wasn't in a book it didn't exist. But now that I am beginning to awake it would appear that I am by no means dreaming and the world is very much here in all its material presence, and only after what seems like a minute do I realize that, of course, I am in Venice where I arrived only last night and had trouble finding my hotel in the ancient darkness. I remember at last now why I came here: disenchanted with living and working like a donkey, rolling boulders uphill, following meaningless, repetitive tasks and rituals, disenchanted with an order of things in which having extirpated the problems of the world people seemed only to have found oblivion in their place and yet rather than find a way out of this oblivion only smothered it with distraction upon distraction. I was living an anxious lie, I knew, and to rid myself of this anxiety left for Venice, the city which has always seemed to promise for me some magnificent but obscure revelation I have yet to decipher for myself. I would like, ambitiously, to find the answers to those questions that so many others out of easy despair or cynicism have given up on and excused themselves from the search only by claiming, with ironic surety, that there weren't any. Of course, it isn't as though I expect some smug, tight little formula, as easy as 2+2=4. Whatever would that prove? No, I expect the kind of divine sunlight which descends on you from cloudless blue, so unanticipated that one hardly knows oneself anymore, the kind of revelatory truth from which there can be no retreat, and accompanied by a Eureka of joy infinitely deeper in its wisdom and knowledge than sadness and despair, the kind able to create worlds from out of itself.

Apart from the motoscarfi there is no traffic noise outside and I can hear only the hollow, stony echoes in the congenial silence. Venice, yes, an envied anomaly, a beautiful contradiction, a fused mutation of East and West where opposites interweave themselves, conjoin, coil around each other like the ribbons of colour spiraling around the mooring posts. Everything, subject and object, stone and sea, the solid and the liquid, mirrors and echoes each other. You can think or imagine or feel anything here. Everyone does it. It's easy.

One day, if only for myself, I should write this all down and make these disjointed thoughts cohere into a presentable order and intelligible unity.

Tired of thought as I lie here staring blankly outwards I try to ascertain my location and time by focusing my gaze on the various objects in the room. I am in my hotel bedroom. There isn't enough light and I can't yet see the Grand Canal through the window, but as I come round to consciousness what light there is directs my eyes to a rose, a crimson rose arising from a translucent Rigadin vase, and with this rose I decide to establish a kind of circular, meditative, Taoist rapport in which the object of meditation is both the singular departure and universal goal. It is dusk and the lemon yellow light is heightening the intensity of the outer petals with a luminescence. I notice how the five outer petals are each divided into two lobes, spiraling into inner petals and how these petals are composed of nanofolds, papilla microphpillae, forming superhydronic surfaces where water droplets cohere but do not readily slide off. Towards the yellow beneath the petals are the five sepals, but with no immediate access for pollination. The rose hips each contain an outer fleshly layer containing what look like dozens of sepals in a matrix of hairs. I know that cultivated roses, unlike original roses, contain no inner petals. The stem prickles are sickle-shaped hooks.

So much for the botanical description, but symbolism and metaphor also permeate the facticity of the flower itself, and no matter how hard I try to extract the physical essence of the rose it is the metaphorical and literary rose that preoccupies me. Life 'finds tongues in trees, books in the running brooks, sermons in stones, and good in everything.'

Begin with the particular, with the modest detail of this rose and allow my ideas to radiate from it, emulating these petals which spiral out to its edge. The rose is a rose is a rose, yes, but the more inscrutably it opposes me in its facticity the more it dares me to penetrate its mystery, and there is no opposing these spectral metaphors and associations that coalesce around it of their own accord. All the poetic and religious examples come to mind: Paradise

Regained, Celestial Bliss, the Passion of Christ, the Holy Grail, the Alchemical Rose, Resurrection, any Desirable Thing, Koranic law, The Magic Circle, the Self, the great 'I' from which the sun shines, and so on. Everything has been said about the rose, but here it is again, inexhaustibly outlasting anything I can say about it, a still half-open book, its inner pages still unread within the deeper recesses of its spiral. But already the darkness is coming and the rose's brilliance is fading.

I know that this trip is a mere stab in the dark, almost an act of desperation and despair, but then again I had to do something, I had to make some kind of move.

It is April, Venice is not yet hot and crowded with tourists and outside I can hear the carefree shouts of children playing in the fondamenta below my window, dream children reminding me of how it might have been for me and how it will be for them, perhaps, in the glorious, inevitable futures they imagine for themselves.

I say to myself that I have come here to look for The Great Revelation but I now know that I have really come here because of Claire when all I see and imagine when I look at the rose is her. So why did I leave her and come all this way? She wanted me to stay and live with her, we were even going to marry at one stage but my friends and family were against it. My mother, especially, for whatever vague, untold reasons of her own, did not approve of her or even like her, and like some jealous matriarchal goddess from mythology she even tried, diabolically I have to say, to undermine me by telling Claire the kind of things about myself I would have been terrified to tell anyone. According to her Claire was too young for me, she was not my type, I was unreliable, and so forth. It is all as tritely fatalistic and Oedipal as any TV drama or romantic novel. But are they right and do they indeed know me better than I do myself, am I the type to commit my life to anyone and am I deceiving myself? No, surely they cannot see her the way I see her. How can they judge her so surely and what is their agenda? How weak and cowardly I was in allowing unknown consequences to intimidate me. Why, as if I was ready to sacrifice all, did I allow myself to take their side rather than Claire's, why would I allow them to decide for me? I remember the very time and day, all sunshine and flowery meadows, when she told me how contemptuous she was of my compliant timidity towards my mother.

Maybe this distance and detachment will, paradoxically, bring me closer to her and to an understanding of what has been happening, I vainly tell myself. Know the personal yet keep to the impersonal, as they say.

If I also came here in the hope of finding the Great Truth, this city is too ambiguous and dreamlike for such easy certainty. Sharply, emphatically vertical, it doesn't allow you to sink into vagueness and escape from yourself, and because it's so compact you can't avoid the way others see you and how you see yourself in regard to them. Too much introspective solipsism is futile here and the city demands you come up with the goods, show yourself, put yourself on display, sort yourself out, confront yourself and yet, even then, because it was itself built on an insubstantial dream it always has a soft spot for the dreamer.

What else can I do now that I have arrived but to leave the hotel and meander around the *calli, fondamente* and *campi*? Here I am, then, at the place where Proust found that his dream had become his own address and the place Nietzsche called 'another name for music.' And yes, I have the sense of treading on notes, crossing bar lines and negotiating scales when I cross the ponti and ascend or descend the steps, pass through the sottoportegi and enter new calli, the lowest notes balanced precariously over the aquatic abyss, the rising pitches of the spires leaping octaves off the scale.

I have been here three times before, but never with Claire. Perhaps if she had come with me it would be different and I could share Venice with her. When I was with Claire I would often think of Venice and was impatient to visit it again, but as she was never one to venture far from home and preferred to dream of far-off places rather than visit them, she didn't want to come. She was always for me, quite literally, the girl from next door, the girl I had was born to know and had known since she was nine, the kind of person people spend their entire lives looking for but never find even after traveling to the far corners of the earth. There was really no distance separating us apart from the hedge at the bottom of the garden, and you could not even say, as one can say of one's first love, that she had opened a door to me when there was no wall and so no door to open in the first place. That, parochial as it sounds, is perhaps how things should have remained with me, but it seemed all too easy and I had always been suspicious of and dissatisfied with whatever seemed easy. I wanted the world and, in the struggle I imagined was necessary for it and for which I had hardened myself, would sell and forfeit almost everything.

I know all about jealousy, about the ugly politics and drama of love, but not love's teleology, its epistemology, its metaphysical dimension.

No, if I can't see Claire, I will look for someone else, perhaps here in Venice.

Venice: the future seen in a dream, or the heaven before they began to call heaven by the name they give it now: the hypothesized future.

This quietness will allow me to listen to myself. It is a city in which I can still hear myself think and allow my thoughts to wander wherever they want. I am less constrained, less intimidated by that world beyond where it often seems necessary to travel long distances to get anywhere and spend disproportionate amounts of energy to do the slightest thing. There is another more sprightly kind of energy here that invigorates you. Being its own kind of joke on the world Venice is funny and you want to laugh along with it. It is a kind of burlesque theatre conspiring against the mundane world and where even a simple transaction of one's stage money, and accompanied by ironic, complicit smiles, transforms itself into a comic parody on the crude wheelings and dealings of that solemn world beyond the lagoon. At the restaurant I overheard a ludicrous conversation of the kind that could only remind me of how I would never show myself again in one of those brightly-lit offices where today all the world's evils are concocted. An American businessman was brashly remonstrating two associates from 'human resources' on the required number of personnel it would be necessary to direct the latest range of plastic homeware they were planning to manufacture Big Time, and because he was becoming aggressively louder with each drink and annoying the other diners, the wife of the restaurant's owner shouted at him from behind the bar to 'back off.' It seems, if I heard correctly, that the subject of this complaint was a female employee he had observed ignoring the guest speakers at a meeting of the company's annual conference the night before as she wrote extraneous notes (was it poetry?) in a notebook she held holding furtively below the tabletop. I can understand how she felt. Why have a business conference in Venice, of all places? The American says 'Let's get out of here' to his colleagues and they are gone.

After two days treading the *calli*, allowing myself to get lost, I have finally returned, coming full circle under the moonlight to the Campo San Fantin at the entrance to the Teatro La Fenice, where I have an espresso at the Restauranto Al Theatro (Why the Latin spelling?). But who is this woman I had seen before twice in the last two days at the table opposite, on the other side of the green latticed divider? I'm sure I saw her two years before when I came to Venice last. I have often seen her striding through this campo and always wondered who she was. Sometimes I have seen her leading groups of tourists. An obscure significance and recognition, although of what, I don't know, attaches itself to my image of her each time she walks by, even if I know this significance has nothing to do with who she really is and with that life of hers about which I can know nothing. But apparently it only takes less than half a second before we recognize a potential soulmate.

She looks like Claire, that's it. She is another version of her, a mirror image, she has the same black hair and that both innocent and knowing vaguely intelligent beauty. She might even be her sister. Or is she the ghost of someone? There are many ghosts in Venice, you can hear their swarming whispers in the night and you accept them as easily as you do your fellow inhabitants in the land of the living. The dead open the eyes of the living, as the old Venetian proverb has it. *I morti verze i oci ai vivi.*

Each time I see her I am more drawn to her, even though I suspect she is way out of my league, a 'heaven so far and fair' that no poor clown, no country bumpkin like me could ever aspire to reach. But at least I know she is a resident here. Could it be that she comes from an old Venetian family? I know she recognizes me, but I have no concern for whether or not she thinks I am following her as you can't be mistaken for a stalker here and if you did decide to stalk someone you always ran the risk of being stalked yourself. It is the mirror-image nature of things in this city, the local joke. Even after a few days in Venice it is impossible if you venture outside long enough not to see people you recognize, impossible not to inadvertently follow them, impossible not to be seen by them. No respecter of personal independence, the city is always exposing you to the chance encounters of others, within this maze everyone runs into each other at some time and you can well understand the convenience or even life-and-death necessity in earlier centuries of wearing masks. Always presided over and guided by the city's ubiquitous spirit, you are never truly a free spirit here, never entirely the master of your own will and where, if you are lost, it is of no consequence when the city can guide you through dozens of other ways to your destination. No need then to force anything, as if Venetians didn't secretly already know that that nothing separates them, that all things in this city of antinomies, this song of opposites finally somehow seem to resolve themselves and reunite. So no hiding from this, no pretense otherwise.

So how to contrive a meeting? As an outsider I am curious, I want to speak to her, partly because she looks like Claire but also because she is exotically and quintessentially Venetian and I am in thrall to her wild, dark eyes. Unlike the tourists who don't, as a rule, dress as the occasion which is Venice would seem to demand, like most Venetians she dresses well and wears a delicate, antique Murano threaded necklace and earrings of pearl and smoky white glass, or Aventurine crystal, as seen, I recall, in paintings of young Venetian women by Tintoretto or Albrecht Dürer, and which I conjecture might perhaps have been left her by an ancient relative. I want to know Venice through its people and I won"t be able to gain any access to its mystery without knowing at least one of them, but it is better not to be impatient and I know that in this city what will be will be and eventuate in its own chosen and canny way.

The same restaurant. There she is again, partly obscured by the divider and the vase of lilacs at her table.

As it happens there is no need to approach her with some contrived excuse for a casual social contact. I realize I don't need to stalk her and I know she comes through the same campo at the same time every day. But who knows what she might think of me, if she thinks of me at all? She is suspicious of, even afraid. Perhaps she thinks I lack principles. I can already see that in her eyes. Over the

centuries Venetians have accustomed themselves to the disillusionment of romance, with perfidious tourists, traders, sailors or traveling merchants who come and go, love and leave. And who knows,
she might, as in the films, surmise I am working for an international criminal organization scouting for another willing recruit, or,
on the other hand, she might think likewise of me, for that matter.
Venice spurns or accept its tourists at its own whim. Most leave,
and only some stay, but for now Venice, it seems, has no immediate
desire to reject me. I am at home here and Venice seems at home
with me.

In my wanderings earlier in the day I found a second-hand copy
of an obscure book amongst disorganized piles of books at the
bookshop Libreria Acqua Alta off the Calle Longa Santa Maria For-
mosa, Castello. Out of curiosity, without searching for any book
in mind, after a helpful conversation with the all-knowing, jovial
owner who, with his beard, blue jersey and marine cap, might have
been a retired sea captain, and a briefer conversation with his gre-
garious tabby cat, who appeared to be supervising the desk, I bought
it. It is a new English translation of the *incombabula Hypnerotomachia
Poliphili* (a romance said to be by Francesco Colonna and a famous
example of early printing. Printed by Aldus Manutius in Venice in
1499, it contains 168 woodcuts showing the scenery: buildings, stat-
ues, gardens, in almost manic detail.

I am at my table reading the *Hypnerotomachia Poliphili* and being
in full view in a public space, can hardly call my life my own. I know
this pretense of writing a letter or reading a book in public will not
stand. You cannot act the solitary in public. If I wanted to read a
book or write I would stay inside without distractions, or at least
only those distractions I might invent for myself. Why else am I
here if I do not wish to see or be seen or to speak with anyone? No, I
might as well be performing on a stage before a vast audience, noth-

ing could be more public and this pretense at preoccupied busyness won't deceive anyone. Now I only await that primordial horror, yes horror, that accompanies the first meeting, the encounter, the plunge into the abyss of that other with whom one already knows one is about to be smitten.

"The Strife of Love in a Dream!" I heard a woman's voice exclaim behind me.

There she is at the next table, indicating with the direction of her gaze the book's cover. She has a look at once sympathetic, quizzical and apprehensive. This time she is wearing a long, lapis lazuli blue dress. Her hair is plaited in the style of Botticelli's Simonetta Vespucci.

I am taken unaware by this intrusion into my suitably public display of privacy and calm solitude. For some infantile reason the old directive for young children enters my head: 'Don't talk to strangers.' But I am not an infant. Let's try to look unsurprised. Or perhaps I am unsurprised and perhaps, after all, in this convoluted city we were destined to meet somehow or another.

"I bought it at the bookshop only yesterday. I don't know much about it. Only that the owner of the bookshop said it was originally printed here in Venice. Do you know it well?"

"I know it. I have a copy myself. It isn't set in Venice but it might have been. Have you seen the woodcuts yet?"

No introductions needed then.

"So you know it."

"It's about a man, Poliphilo, who dreams he meets a girl, only to find that it is his former girlfriend, and who leads him on a tour through buildings, landscapes and gardens. It's a book on architecture. The man loses her and re-finds her again. Polia, she is called. Her name means 'many things.'"

"You are alone?"

"Yes. A lone tourist in Venice."

"Megio soli che mal compagnadi. It is better to be alone than to be in bad company. An old Venetian proverb. I'm not bad company, am I?"

"No! Of course not! Would you like to sit here?"

"What's your name? Che nòme gasto?"

So she even speaks Venetian, she knows the dialect. I tell her my name.

"What's yours?"

"Marina."

The name couldn't be more appropriate, of course. Soon we are seated together.

"You live here?" I ask. "Are you Venetian?"

"I was not born here, but, yes, I am fifth generation Vèneta. I'm a tour guide. I lead small dedicated groups of tourists around all six sestieri and show them the more discrete and less accessible places."

"So it goes without saying that you know Venezia well."

"I know Venezia as well as anyone can. San Marco, Dorsoduro, San Polo, Santa Croce, Cannaregio and Castello. Sometimes even I get lost. A building that was there one week ago seems to disappear, I can't find it anywhere, and when I thought I knew one calle, another building, unknown to me, appears there as if from nowhere, like magic, like the castle in an old fairy tale."

"Have you been here before?"

"A few times over the years. This will be my fourth time."

"What really attracts you to Venice? As if I needed to ask. But why do you like it so much? What is it to you? Is it the buildings, the art, the history? What is it? "

I don't tell her that I am hoping for the big revelation, of course."In my eyes it's the most impossibly beautiful city in the world," I tell her, using the tried-and-ready description, but I try to convey how something in me, perhaps even something aquatic in my own soul, seems to correspond with this city barely suspended above the water lapping around and beneath you and where, even if you are always one step away from drowning, your spirits find a special buoyancy and lightness you could never find in the world beyond the lagoon. I am more human here, more myself and, unoppressed by the modern world's methodical project of dehumanizing us all, less guarded and apologetic about being myself.

But I still don't know how far to go on this. I hope I don't sound too nonsensical.

"Perhaps I can join your tour one day? I have never been taken on a guided tour by a genuine Venetian," I said, stressing the word 'genuine.'

"Yes, of course, I would be happy to take you on a tour. But I am not due for another group tour until the 12th. My associate is standing in for me. Perhaps I can take you on a tour myself?"

"Why not? I have nothing else to do. I'm a tourist, aren't I? How much do I owe you?"

Being a good, suitably venal Venetian she says: "One hundred Euros.... How about that?"

I won't say no. It's done. Not unreasonable. I pay the hundred Euros.

When I am with her I am everyone, and when I was everyone with everyone I was no one.

She trusts me, I trust her, I trust myself with her. It is usually only in films and novels that the apparently innocent stranger is later unmasked as an international drug smuggler or arms dealer on the lookout for a new recruit, but we aren't in a film or novel and she will be my guide, my Ariadne leading me through the city, she will initiate me into the labyrinth of Venice's mysteries and show me *l'île inconnue* that everyone knows or think they know. My will shall not be my own, yes, but it always got in the way of things, anyway. With the fee paid it will all be fun and games, with no strings attached.

The wise old man, the Geppetto, the inflexible, knowing father, the disenchanted romantic in me, my Freudian superego would like to say: don't do it, don't involve yourself with her, don't be like Pinnochio and tell the old lies about yourself simply for effect. But he's always in the way of everything, the old killjoy. Is it that I think she will steal my virtue? But I have no virtue to steal. I will, though, try to tell the truth about myself to her, even despite the lies we often tell to others to preserve any relationship with another, even if we are compelled to say whatever enters our heads, however false, if only to fill the silence.

In the earnestly efficient world beyond the lagoon you can so resent being deflected from the straightened path of your worldly concerns that you can barely waylay or talk freely with anyone for more than a minute and everyone invents excuses for absenting themselves. But what place do straight lines have here when every canal and calle curves back on itself, and what in Venice might I be deflected from? From my direct path from A to Z? But I have no one path from A to Z. Everything is circular, you end where you began.

If love wants the protecting walls of paradise, it also wants yearning infinity, and in this feminine, maternal city, the shot silk colours of water and sky countenancing the hardness of its stones, the infinity of the sea is never far from one's doorstep, and as the Taoist sages would say, all rivers run to it, all things are born from and end in it, and the soft always overcomes the hard.

To the visitor, if not to its remaining inhabitants, everything and everyone here dissolves into image and myth. Tycoons, business people, politicians, tourists: it all becomes theatre.

From the Accademia Bridge and on to San Polo and the Goldoni museum. This is where farce, opera and, for that matter, soap opera were invented. Da Ponte, Carlo Goldoni. Drama built around gossip and intrigue. El petegolo xe na spia senza paga. Gossip is an unpaid spy. After this it is on to the Museo Rezzonico, through Dorsoduro, the Chiesa di San Sebastiano, and onto the Basilica di Santa Maria della Salute. We don't take the vaporetto. She is showing me hidden gardens, inscriptions, sculptures, carvings, monuments, fountains, monsters, mythical beasts, images from my own nightmares, of my own crooked desires from the past. Without having to regain her bearings she knows where she is going, and leads me through Calle del Campanile, Locanda Ca' Foscari, Vigill fel Fuoco, Calle Foscari, Calle Cappeller, Calle dele Boteghe, San Barnaba, Calle del Tragehto to The Accademia, and on through Calle della Chiesa, calle Lanza, cal Le Del bastion, Calle di Mezzo, Rio Terra Saloni, to San Giorgio Maggiore. The broken lime plaster stucco, the crumbling but nevertheless yet somehow durable brick walls. Later in the day it is up the Grand Canal to Ca' d'Oro with the St. Sebastian by Mantegna and the inscription: Nihil nisi divinum stabile est. Caetera fumus (Nothing is stable if not divine. The rest is smoke).

Marina the tour guide begins her spritely monologue:

Research shows that Venice has subsided a total of 15-16 centimetres since 1900. Just 3-4 centimetres are accounted for by natural subsidence, while 12 cm can be traced back to the pumping of ground water from aquifers below the city, until the Sile aqueduct was constructed in 1975. This sinking has been coupled with a 7-8 centimetre rise in global water levels, allowing for an overall change of 23 centimetres relative to sea level. While this may not seem like very much, it actually represents a very significant change....

Later we stop to nibble on snacks, bacaro, and tramezzini, those giant sandwiches with the crusts cut off, filled with tuna, ham, cheese, tomatoes and mozzarella.

Marina continues her monologue, the one she must surely know by heart:

The Chiesa di San Sebastiano (or The Church of Saint Sebastian) is a 16th-century Roman Catholic church located in the Dorsoduro sestiere. Paolo Veronese spent three periods between 1555 and 1570 decorating various parts of the interior of San Sebastiano. This included paintings, ceiling canvases and frescoes on the nave and altar walls. Veronese also decorated parts of the sacristy, the choir, as well as completing the organ decorations and a large altarpiece. The paintings behind the choir depict the life of St Sebastian to whom the church is dedicated....

She says: "I think there is something of Sebastiano in you. The scourged Christ, the man with the broken heart, *ecce homo,* the man of sorrows. You 'suffer the outrageous slings and arrows of outrageous fortune' like Sebastiano but somehow you know you will come back to life again. Suffering has strengthened you and turned the lead of suffering into gold. There is something in you of Pierrot, the sad clown."

Yes, without telling her anything about myself she seems to know me better than I do, she senses everything about me and even seems to know my own past. But who is she? I am divided between the two questions: the who and the what. Who is she beyond my own perception of her, what does she represent to me, and what is my own little self versus the many possible selves of Marina? Yes, Marina is Polia, 'many things.' Like Venice itself, Marina in all her volatile, liquid reality understands me beyond words and language and my own relative hardness of soul is no match for her. If Marina is a water nymph with all the eloquence of the spirits, it is I who, like Pinocchio, am thick and solid, I who am a blockhead. But I too want to be as liquid and fearless as water.

Abstract speculations, yes, but what in the world isn't abstract and can't be abstracted from it and isn't the world fabricated from insubstantial, invisible abstractions, isn't the world a script of sorts?

Abstraction is inherent in nature herself, in those Bosons, for example, that lend the universe its mass and substance.

Problems. Is everything a problem for me? But are there any problems to solve in the first place?

But it is no good, it wasn't supposed to happen this way. What began perhaps as a game, a holiday pastime, is turning into love, into old-fashioned, romantic love and perhaps I should pack my bags and go home before I damage her affections any further. How would it all end? I can't, in all seriousness, allow myself to play with her affections like this when I know I will leave Venice sooner or later. Perhaps I am far too old for her, and I could almost be her father, for that matter. Despite my best scruples, like a lapsed puritan I have broken every vow and stricture I made to myself when I once told myself I was never going to be enamoured of anyone again, I am 'in love,' as they say, I have taken my own bait, I am caught in my own trap. How then to extricate myself from this trap, assuming I even want to extricate myself from it? To evade her would be, as always, yet another evasion of myself, an escape to nowhere, and it would seem sad, anyway, to both leave her and leave Venice now. Leaving now would seem callous, as callous as popping a child's balloon, Venice herself would be saddened and offended, and, anyway, who knows what is happening behind the scenes of fate, so to speak, who am I to know my own place in the machinations of fate and where it may be leading me, and how should I be expected to know what is true or false in this theatrical city of deception and deceit from which I am no more exempt than anyone else? On the other hand, it might be wiser to let events unfold and develop in their own way, to let Venice articulate what it wants from us in its own time. As a Venetian she already knows all there is to know about deceit, she knows how things always are here with so many people coming and going, meeting each other for a few hours or days, making false promises and never seeing each other again. She wasn't born yesterday. I can't alter or hurry time, time is God and I am comfortable with it, I can live with it. Magic, yes, let magic have its way. Why should I spoil it all? The magic is all I know and can ever know.

I must see Marina again, I must see her every day, everything depends on it, Marina is Venice and Venice is Marina.

We are seeing each other every day at the same place.

One day, with the candour only she knows how to convey without embarrassment, she says we we may have known each other in another time and I reply that yes, it seems that way, I have the same sensation, but I don't return the candour and add that she is my saving, resolving *Deus ex machina,* a divine emissary from some more exalted sphere.

One days she says: "But there is someone else, isn't there? I can tell. Someone else at home. Come on, it's all right, you can tell me."

But there is always someone else.

"Someone else? Yes, if you want to know, there is Claire. Her name is Claire." I can't lie. She would know I was.

"Why isn't she with you now? Why didn't you bring her with you?" is the obvious question.

I tell her that she prefers staying at home, that she isn't much of a traveler, and that is true enough.

"How long have you known each other?"

"Since childhood."

"A long romance then."

"Romance? I don't know. We were friends. She made me laugh."

"Could you ever live in Venice?"

I tell myself the idea would be preposterous.

"I would like to, I tell her. I have always dreamed of living here."

I am beginning to doubt my way of seeing the world, I want to disown my own stupid, cynical cleverness when I used to think that the I, the laughable I, small and parochial, could ever exist and have any kind of meaning without another 'I.' The inner voice is not the only voice, not the last word. I should be more honest and realistic with myself and others.

It's time to ask the inevitable question and convey to her more precisely my interest in her. If I don't say something soon we will run the risk of passing each other by, carried off by time in our separate directions and never to see each other again. It's time to reach out and bridge the infinitely parallel lines that separate us, time to find out if she really feels anything for me at all and we are not to carry on as actors merely pretending and lying to one another.

Crassly, I ask her if she has a friend, if she is 'with someone.'

"I am married! You didn't notice my ring?"

So now we know. I didn't notice. A vast crevice opens in the paving stones at my feet and I am about to sink into the dark oblivion of the lagoon.

"We are married, and yet I barely see him now. I have lost any feelings I had for him. One day we will leave each other. He's always traveling, like most people today. He's a civil engineer, he designs bridges and buildings around Italy and Europe. All the work is outside Venice. I, like you, left someone I once loved, only to marry for convenience, for money, for security and, I have to admit, simply to please family and friends. They thought he was right for me. I made the same mistake. I regret marrying him."

So now we know. Is he then to be the flashy Harlequin to my Columbine? Nevertheless, I ask her if I can see her again.

"Yes. Let's see each other tomorrow here, at noon."

So what kind of game, if any, will we be playing from this moment on?

She is interested in me, certainly, and perhaps in some way she likes me, although I am blind when it comes to reading other people's signals in such matters, and even if I am not so vain to presume or expect affection or even respect from anyone. Could we ever live here together? But the idea seems absurd. How could we ever live with each other, cooped up together like cats? And what would I do with no qualifications for working here? Clean toilets? Now I know why she won't reveal her address. She is familiar with strangers such as myself. There have been too many broken hearts in this city of traders and tourists, too many who come and go never to see each other again. But she tells me this with a shrug, without anger or embarrassment or awkwardness, throwing the matter away as inconsequential.

Do I want to escape this dream or remain here in it?

I dreamed last night that after celebrating our union with a brief but heavenly embrace in an ancient temple, she faded away into the mute, infinite darkness, and I awoke.

Joy burns itself through the silence.

The 'I' is the source of light.

Everyone is a traveler. But everything is travel nowadays, is it not?

Does she think I am rich? Does she want my money? Or perhaps she is rich herself and thinks it is I who am merely after her money.

I tell her my own doubts and turmoils but soon my easy, insouciant skepticism begins to irritate her. She calls me stupid and almost pities me as she would a child. To her the order and structure of the world, in which I see only hopeless, chaotic failure, is manifest and visible to any child. But the world, I counter like an idiot, is absurd. There's nothing absurd about it, she counters in return, and there is no such thing as chaos. Everything, she explains carefully like a priestess to a simple novice, is fixed, providential and designed to lead us towards the source of that light which pervades everything.

But if there is no chaos and everything is providential, have we been led here to meet each other? If so, why, and what can we do about it? Have I found The One? Is she, rather than Claire, the One, the All, the Revelation, my Absolute?

The coming of the new, unprecedented event, the unknown opposed to the already known, the disruptor of the mundane progress of time: it's what everyone wants and expects. But how to tell if it has the stamp of truth and you haven't deluded yourself?

Today in San Polo I see her walking briskly along with a man at her side. She doesn't see me. I only assume it is her husband or boyfriend. He looks saturnine, not grand at all, not her type, I would have said. What does she see in him? Or is it only that he has money? But what a mundane conjecture. I am already jealous, but I don't want her to know it and don't even want her to know I saw her with him. I don't want jealousy poisoning everything.

Already I am betraying myself with my own anger and impatience. Who is he?

But this infernal, internal monologue. Why don't I act on these thoughts, why don't I ask her? Shall I openly declare more than a simple interest or curiosity in her, shall I tell her, dare I say it, that I love her?

Is she the truth, and all the rest lies?

A stranger to myself, I don't know myself. But what makes me think I have a self to know? Do I want to know myself?

The things I say to people, how badly I do it, the phraseology repeated continuously like a script, the banalities and platitudes I curse myself for the moment I utter them, and the lies we tell to maintain ourselves together. There's no end to it. But if I were to stop telling lies and be honest what would happen? No doubt I would loose everything.

Other people are bright, but I alone am in the dark.

One day when we are speaking about lies and honesty and the social proprieties of telling lies, she says: "You know the old Venetian proverb? *A dir busie ocor bona memoria.* Who tells lies must have a good memory."

She tells me she inherited the small apartment she shares with her husband. It is in San Polo and has a partial view of the Grand Canal, but she does not have money and one day, she supposes, she will need to sell it for a tidy sum to a foreigner, *un foresto.* There is Venice and the world that is not Venice, the world beyond, and now that the Beyond has invaded Venice will there ever be a truly native Venetian left?

She tells me today that her husband has returned to France, where he has a new job. He had to return for a few days to organize things and, according to him, 'gather together some papers.'

So there is hope after all.

Happiness, or rather joy and beauty: that's all there is, when all is said and done.

What can we say to each other? I can't understand her, I can't read her, even if she can read my deepest soul despite my dubious, preposterous confessions. Perhaps she has a file on me, perhaps she has the dirt on me, perhaps she is a spy, but in her almost maternal way I sense that she would forgive and understand anything about myself I would otherwise try to hide from her.

I am almost ready to tell her then and there, despite my own best scruples and tempting absolute ridicule, that I want to marry her, but of course I don't, I am only daydreaming. She will say no, I can't marry you, and already I can hear the inevitable reply as she laughs or giggles in my face. But I ask her if I can see her more often, if we can be, well, dare I say it, 'friends'.

"Friends? We can be friends. Why not? As for anything more: no. And can you hold that against me? There are too many Venetian heartbreaks around and for centuries we have learnt to be on our guard with our visitors. You will leave Venice one day, I know you will."

No, she is right, I could never live here, I would be an imposter. And could she live anywhere else but in Venice? There is Venice and the *terra ferma* beyond, the world of the foreigners, the ones who aren't Venetian.

I don't know whether or not I am lying to her or to myself, or both. Are my strongest affections for Marina or Claire? Am I even in love? How do I know if I love anyone? Do I even believe in love? I might as well be playing a beefy character in a TV soap drama, tragically caught between his love of two women. Perhaps I am being false to myself, perhaps I am indeed 'falser than vows made in wine' and my feelings amount to nothing more than mere jealousy of her husband and the world she belongs to, the world to which I have no entry, no key. Callously I allow her to see the photo of Claire I carry in my wallet and she recognizes and acknowledges with a glance the similarity to herself.

"What does it matter in the end what your relatives think? Or is it that you have too much to loose by following your own promptings? *Hai mai le dici che amavi?* Tell me: Did you ever tell her you loved her?"

I realize that I never declared any such thing to Claire and having known her so many years I had innocently assumed she knew or surmised we shared the kind of telepathic communications that would render such a declaration unnecessary. Must we declare everything to be understood?

"Tell her. They will come around in the end, they will appreciate her, see her the way you see her. You found her, she found you. It's all staring you in the face. Everything you want has been staring out at you but you are unaware of it. Go back to her. She's there, waiting for you, she's the answer, the end of your search. You probably think you are in love with me, but for you I am only a passing mood, an image, a caprice, a fictitious character, a cypher. You don't know me, I hardly know you and when you see who I really am I am sure you will soon tire of me and I will seem like anyone else. Anyway, I can see from the photo that I am only a substitute for Claire. I am not what you think I am. I can tell you this, because I made the same mistake you made. I once left someone because my parents didn't like him or approve of him for whatever of reasons of their own, and now, look where I am, married to someone I barely see, someone I clearly don't love, and yet even today I am still thinking about that first man I met and left behind years ago."

Yes, she is right, perhaps Marina is only a mood and I merely the manipulated plaything of this mood but, after all, isn't everything a matter of mood, no matter how objective we think we are, and isn't Marina herself, if not a mood, then an ongoing mode or way of being? Perhaps to find out that Claire is the One, the very One, the All, I had to first come here and meet Marina. Yes. I believe now I will return to Claire, if she is still there and if she is not indifferent to me. It is she, after all, who has remained with me over these years, it is she who has been the presiding deity over my life's comings and goings. How little do we recognize what is too vast for us, how ignorant we are of what is most ours. And perhaps, anyway, it was even Claire herself in some mysterious way who directed me to Marina for this purpose. But what will she say to me when I get home, if she is there at all?

Marina is undoing my ideas of the self and what it is to be a self, she is one of those rare types, an ageless rebuke to the modern, an incarnation of the World Soul, someone who can see through and beyond today's duplicity and fragmentation and into the oceanic unity surrounding and supporting everything, she, like Isis with her Osiris in the underworld, is reassembling me again to make me new.

I ask her again a few days later if I can see her once more. Yes, she says, and we take the motoscarfo to the Lido and stroll along the Lungomare Guglielmo Marconi, passing the Excelsior and the Hotel des Bains and turning up busy Granviale Santa Maria Elisabetha, where we stop for coffee at one of the many outdoor restaurants lining it.

To stave off the nullity left in the place of the sacred did I merely substitute it with idle chatter and exaggerated drama? Perhaps I should take stock, set myself up in some humble dwelling somewhere in my own fourfold world of earth, sky, mortals and divinities, perhaps I should cultivate my garden and stop traveling so much. The technology of flight is admirable, but traveling can indeed narrow the mind and as someone once said it is sometimes more poetic to stay at home and dream of distant places rather than travel to them.

Apropos of the Danish philosopher: confusing the categories of the aesthetic and the real, had I found the fully aesthetic life wanting because the real could never meet its high ideals? Was I such the foolish romantic living the aesthetic life, forever chasing momentary pleasures and distractions in the pursuit of some distant, impossible perfection? But as for the fully ethical life, that too would have been wanting. Too serious, for one thing, and what would anyone's life amount to without the aesthetic dimension? No, in the end either way without the other is false, it costs too much, it breaks your heart, it's impossible, you become inhuman, despising everything and everyone. The good and the beautiful, the actual and the ideal are not mutually exclusive but reconciled in a higher synthesis of the finite and the infinite....and so on and so on.

Somewhat pompously and pendantically I disclose to Marina these secondhand ideas of mine on the actual and the ideal, on the fall, on the Ground of Being, but she replies: "But we have never fallen. We forget that we only pretend we have, and we loose ourselves, playing hide-and-seek with ourselves only as a wager to ourselves that we can re-find ourselves. We think we are lost until one day, years hence, from out of nowhere, we see that all along we were happily ensconced in paradise without knowing it."

We travel the world but there is no avoiding beauty and joy, they are everywhere, following us, facing us, and no matter what befalls you they will always find you in the end and have the last word. It is only because joy is too heavy for us that we try to stave it off for a lighter, easier, more entertaining way of being.

The sun is rising on this all-too-solid dream of mine and ageless Marina is vanishing, she will disappear from me as I try, like Pierrot, to clutch at the impossible moon. I think I should exit now, but gently, with an appropriate gesture of useless, courtly grace.

April 25, the date both of the Festa di San Marco and the Festa del Bocolo. The feast days of the patron saint of Venice, the Rosebud or Blooming Rose Festival and Liberation Day are celebrated in and around Piazza San Marco. Tradition has it that if you're in Venice on that day men should present their partner with a long-stemmed red rose, and you will find plenty of florists ready to sell you one.

I duly buy her a red rose at an inflated price and present it to her. She receives it graciously and presents me with a kiss that is not so resigned as I might have expected but almost passionate and with even a hint of that same desperation that hinted at some dark power oppressing her. But a moment later, not to be undone, and modifying the Venetian tradition, she draws from her bag her own red rose and presents me with it.

Yes, I have indeed been chasing an idea, a phantom, and yet has she not shown me the way to Claire, the one who never travels and who from the beginning was always present and steadfast at the very centre of my own provincial little neighbourhood where I once dreamed my own imaginary Venice, my own unattainable *île inconnue?*

"Perhaps you will return to Venezia one day and bring Marina with you."

Claire tells me I could do with some new clothes. A nice new suit, for example, would be a start, and she leads me to a shop where she believes I can find the right one. The big boy suit I choose off the rack happens to fit me perfectly and as I look into the gilt-framed, Rococo mirror I hardly believe I am real, someone almost different, someone spared from one ignominious life to be granted a promising new one, someone unafraid to look the world squarely in the face again without looking away from it. The suit seems to bestow on me a quiet surety of strength superior to the wooden rigidity of former times. Yes, I, Pinocchio, have grown up and become a real-life human.

Time, I am sure of it now, will unfold in its own time and answer every yearning in some blue, sunlit eternity well beyond old killjoy death.

I have awoken, and if perhaps all that happened here in Venice was a dream after all and should remain with me as such, then let's keep it that way. Better to let go of it all and preserve what happened in the dreamworld where it truly belongs. Now that I understand, and because you can only see what you truly understand, I can see again, and I can speak to Claire without the old hesitancy that would have prompted me in earlier days to retreat into sad silence. Time to speak, time also to come back to earth, but an earth that will never be the same again, an earth more uncanny, more foreign and luminous than I would ever have imagined.

Fate and the Philosopher

Speak of what I know, I tell myself, but what do I, as a humble philosopher, know and what can I ever know? More often than not it seems I am searching for knowledge only to shore myself against the unfamiliar and inexplicable. I might tell myself, like Socrates, that the one thing I know is that I know nothing, but am I not merely being disingenuous in so choosing to play the ignorant simpleton? How can I even know, for that matter, that I know nothing, when perhaps this knowledge was already embedded in my soul at birth and how can it be that I know nothing when, a long time ago, one autumn day, I was sure as sure as I could ever be that I glimpsed that impossible, insouciant Absolute, smiling and shining like a beautiful woman from beyond the dour cloud of unknowing hanging over us? It is true that, if asked at the time, I could not have said what it was I knew and yet, if I had not been asked, it nevertheless seemed that somehow, inexplicably, I knew and was on the edge of uncovering, or should I say remembering, that thing of precious import radiantly obvious and self-evident in its truth but which I had somehow forgotten or neglected to remember over the years. It even seemed that all of nature already knew, but that it was only perhaps language itself that did not know and it was only the jumble of words in my head preventing me from deciphering the meaning at hand. And today, again, more than ever, after staring down at G on his hospital deathbed, the finality of his death as mundane as the room's sterile utilitarian surroundings and the grey expanse of car park you could see from the window, the question arose in the face of such finality as to what that precious jewel of truth beyond this horizon of swarming particulars and hardened abstractions might be. Without it seemed I would be left with nothing to speak of and it was thus befallen on me, if I was to have a life upon which I could look down without regret, to know again this one thing subject to no other knowledge. Knowing this might release me from this obdurate striving, this fixation which had been pursuing me like a madness and I might learn to forget and move onward again. It is time then, once and for all, to set all other considerations aside and get to the heart of the matter. If I knew what I knew then I should remain silent, but not knowing I must speak or at least write notes, if only to myself. Yes, it's time to stop prevaricating, there's no time to loose.

Yes, I remember that glimmer from so long ago it pains me to think about it, that moment when, in a twinkling of an eye, someone else, or a voice within, told me that it wasn't all an arbitrary dream and there was an obstinate, founding solidity within or beyond or behind it all and I could almost believe that I was not altogether ignorant and deluded, not quite in the dark. I am certain of it now, all mysticism, all madness aside, that something happened that I am unable to renounce or ignore, I was vouchsafed a perception, a glance, the gates opened on... On what, on what did this epiphany open? A ravishing image of paradise, the realm of the God and hundreds of such poetic or theological metaphors come to mind. Perhaps those Gods we have supposedly banished are returning through the back door to play a trick on me, if only to remind me that they have never disappeared and cannot be spirited away so easily. Who knows? Whatever it was, something momentarily intervened from nowhere with the full force of surprise to supersede all else and promise to set everything aright, to alter the past, to illuminate all that was meaningless and incomplete, to repair the irreparable, to redeem, to contradict every blundering wrong and prove that oblivion itself doesn't have the last word and all is indeed for the best. Yes, it was a moment bursting its seams with limitless, almost lethal joy, but full also with the promise of knowing the very source of such a joy. I could swear, contrary to my trained uncertainties in such matters, contrary to the principle of verifiability that only statements empirically verifiable or logically necessary have any meaning at all, that I had almost touched the summit of the Hegelian absolute. I was about to turn away from my own, telling myself that there may be something wrong, that I had made a mistake, that I was deceived, but no, I could see with a kind of precision the Big Picture, the pattern and order of all things with everything fell into place and all as it should be, and it seemed I had lived only for this moment and could now make peace with the world.

But already I am struggling for words, loosing traction, saying too much and too quickly, and all this won't convince anyone, let alone myself. Better start once more from the beginning and take each step as it comes. This is the only possible way to proceed, otherwise it will all be false. Begin then from this moment, explicate from this founding origin, from the original proposition: the absolute, the Big One, the universal constant, Hegel's Absolute Knowing, the Truth, the Spirit that knows itself, the Ground of Being, Atman. Why not? Nothing less than this is merely fragmentary. Time to take the issue by the throat, and don't let it go. It's now or never. Forget the small stuff, forget arbitrary details, particulars, the distracted skirting over surfaces. Yes, it's the great sovereign, bubbling, overflowing source itself I'm after. Why pretend otherwise, why settle for anything less?

I must prune the pink Rugosa roses, and if not cut back the Coprosma trees, as much as I admire their glazed leaves, will spoil the vista of the rocky coastline, of Rangitoto Island's greyish green, symmetric slopes, of the porcelain blue sea and the infinite spaces beyond these babbling, perverse dialectics. Ah, this sea view! Perfection itself! Why am I inside with these morbid thoughts when the sun is shining its heart out? Madness. But imperative again to make meaning of this scene. There is something questionable about such perfection. No point in denying it signifies something. It does, it does, perhaps more than it can promise, but I must must somehow piece it all together and make sense of it or everything up till now will have been pointless, a waste. It's the past's only hope. Back then to the words, back to the search, the research. Put all other considerations aside, make a space for yourself, take your time and set this truth of yours to work.

The absolute appeared asking, riddling: can you explain me, can you say what I am? I was unable to answer, and the door to the rose garden closed as soon as opened, leaving an intimation, a glimmer. Perhaps, to prolong its presence long enough to take possession of this proffered knowledge, it would have been enough for me, if not to answer its question, at least, in turn, to ask it a question, the right question. But how, at that early age, were you to know how to formulate it? And moreover, because it left you without voice you were unable to pose the question, even when you knew that what you had seen was infinitely more profound and significant than the darkness commonly regarded as the reservoir of truth. Time then to ask and have done with it. Everything comes back to this glimmer, to this final clue without which nothing holds together, nothing fits. Knowledge or no knowledge, all meaning, all the possibilities of a new life are conditional on this summoning light diminishing into the darkness again, leaving behind the question still unanswered to this very day. All since then has been a constant falling away, a lingering, unforgiving curse for years now, a soft, airless evil smothering the land, a lethargy, a hundred-year sleep as in the fairy tale, and a lingering sadness over this vision of how things should be but would never be again. What it left over in the way of understanding is so little I barely knew what to do with it.

Much time lost then since you fell from that distant star and decided, with youthful ambition, to wager all on answering the riddle of this great, shiny Absolute hanging in the void, as intractably near and distant as any object, beyond the comatose, vacuous suburbs, this Word comprehending all words and making a grandiose sense of it all. But will I then find an opening through this obscurity, or am I to go in circles chasing this doubtless lunatic, monstrous vision, this Cheshire cat, this sphinx, this Mona Lisa of an enigma, all lost to me, all in vain, and succumb like a miserable moth to the darkness again? All that only for this? Or is it better to forget such speculation, to give it all up now as an embarrassing vice and resign myself to the modest, domestic confines of the here and now, to the quiet life as they call it, to take each day as it comes and comfort myself that it was indeed all a vain delusion, a preposterous madness? There is no doubt that because of this obsession everything has been going to seed, that I have neglected practical affairs and any human sympathy. And what is it that you want in the end but the ideal nowness of things in their untouched, carefree noise and chatter, the seasons in their multifarious colours, the scent of celestial flowers, a day without anxiety for the future and without guilt for all missed or left undone? The end of art is peace and silence. But do I really want that now? Isn't that too soon? It would be somehow tedious, like an overlong holiday in the country, and I would be merely be putting things off. No, if only for the sake of feeling something again, I want the return of the old drama, the old romance, the old griefs and heartbreaks. Feeling. That's it, that's it when it comes down to it. Feeling comes first, no denying it. Knowledge or no knowledge, truth or no truth, despite all the dangers I want to feel something again. And yes, I believe I am feeling something again. Wasn't it that rigid, misplaced stoicism in the face of every onslaught that held me back from asking the question in the first place? Having renounced love for telling me false things and sold my soul for the dubious benefits of knowledge and experience, I had almost forgotten what love was.

Everything would be less difficult without the enticement of this glimmer, but there is no going back, no other way out, it's either that or nothing, I have come too far to stop now. There will be no rest from it all, no return to that magical Place and Time, to that little garden with the singing stream and the flowers scented with the promise of paradise until I have addressed the mystery of this question or at the very least found the beginning of an answer, even if this answer should raise more questions than it solves. They say everything comes and goes, nothing lasts, it's a mutable world, a phantasm, love fades and once more you are the plaything of that chance and circumstance which, only a moment before, this love seemed on the point of transcending and rending null and void. Imperative then to understand the significance of that moment. Yes, indeed, I will wager everything, even at the risk of making myself ridiculous in the light of these times when people laugh mercilessly at such brazen leaps of faith, that one day I will look out on the world again without fear and, like Faust, say to the passing moment "How fair thou art, if only you would last, if you could only return eternally!" But it goes without saying that such peace must be earned, like second innocence, like recovered purity of soul, and the only way is to pass through the doorway to the fickle future, despite the cautionary 'abandon all hope' message above it, and only then would I allow myself to surrender to fate and happily dissolve into the ether, a blissful smile on my face. That is the only way you will find your precious Absolute, if at all.

Act. I must act. Dare I say it? Yes I do. In the beginning was the act. Have more faith in yourself and reject these cheap doubts born of this overly skeptical and prudent age. Much more fruitful to cease endlessly entertaining this spirit of doubt, time to be more serious, despite the world's ridicule. You are only misleading yourself with this irritable reaching after fact and reason. Yes, prone as I am to mock anyone who claims certainty in things, when all is said and done I am not one to take perverse delight in contrariness, in disputatious syllogism. Eternity deflates all such sophistry and always has the last laugh. Forget logic, if you can call it that, forget reason and attend in all humility to your own lowly heart. It has its own reasons not to be set aside, not to be trifled with. Let it find its own replies to your interminable questions, let it heal you. Logical argument is no use here at all when nothing, finally, can be proved with it. Yes, nothing is clear and certain (but is such a statement true, is it a certainty that there is no certainty? All this is hopelessly tautological. 'Uncertainties now crown themselves assured') and if even in the self-enclosed world of mathematics and number they have already demonstrated this, there might well be a certainty or at least an understanding I could claim for myself, if not for others. Yes, there could be a feeling, a moment of astonishment if you like, if nothing more, by which I could say that I knew and understood something, the feeling of an ultimate ground of being, or an origin, or homecoming, or affirmation, or chordal resolution, the air palpitating with harmonious music. This not to be dismissed. The white flower of purity and truth is somewhere out there, no denying it, let that be decided, and it could easily be taken from me by my own neglect in pursuing and examining this matter, by the very idea that it was a delusion and nothing more. Yes, there is indeed something crucially missing, something vital without which no meaning is possible, and without which it can not be said I have partaken of life's great feast. The world marches merrily and purposely on and none of all this unproductive perfection is mine. But what was it, what was the event that severed me from all this, what was it that set me spinning out of control, without bearings?

Yes, after all such wanderings, still haunted by this quandary. Thoughts, voices caught in their incessant, obsessive flow centre on an invisible object of speculation whose presence is yet indicated by the outline of the void it leaves. Vague, disjointed, obsessive dictates from somewhere else, mumbling intimations, conversations, ghostly phrases, speculations emerging and trailing off again, won't let go. They filled my head today as I strolled by the row of olive trees (what are olive trees doing here in this suburb?) and the brick and tile church, its spire pointing to outer space, the scent of the lavender hedge lining its frontage of brick wall divided, I noticed for the first time, into a series of slender cement columns, each with a trefoil relief at the apex. But why am I registering such picturesque details unrelated to anything, with no meaning and why make such prosaic, pedestrian observations when there is no reason in this unpredictable, contrary world why the skies should not at any moment open out in joyous, iridescent glory, the cherubs and angels singing Hallelujah. There is no getting over it.

But heaven forbid, stop this plunge into darkness and establish that you are not so presumptuous as to claim for yourself the authority of divine revelation. I would do well to remind myself of that! Others, perhaps everyone for that matter, have been witness to such glimmerings. They are everywhere it seems, as all the books tell us. That has to be said at the very least to establish things.

But where was I, where is all this going? More avoiding the issue, more procrastination. This idle circularity, this infernal solipsism is pointless, laughable, sordid, the very story of my life. But what is beyond it? That is the question. That is what you must secure for yourself. Calm yourself then and retrace your steps. Less hysteria and more stoicism called for. Stop the clock. Less hurry, slow down, lengthen the tempo. One distorts things, one descends into hysteria by siding with a mood. Mustn't get carried away, mustn't get ahead of myself. And important also to be precise, at the very least resist easy vagueness and try to maintain a modicum of clarity and grace under pressure. Best to return then to the beginning, start from scratch, wipe the blackboard clean of the jumble of prejudices and wrong inferences reached over the years, the smudged traces of truth and meaning, and on the blackness chalk in some questions, even a few tentative propositions, a few fragments and notes, search for a few clues which might, as in a detective story, fall into place, all the answers to the crossword puzzle not only found but spelling out in one sentence the secret to the universe? But even if you are left only with questions - who knows? - perhaps these fragments might even cohere and amount to some kind of truth. 'In your nothing might the all be found?' Quite. But then left with this alchemical *prima materia*, where to begin, how to begin, or must I advance blindly, as one lost?

Perhaps it would be more fruitful here to allow yourself the freedom of dialogue with yourself as though you were staging yourself and diverting your bias from the abstract, objective analysis of the external world to direct it to the background of your own life. Not what philosophers are wont to do but could well be good for them if only they knew it. But nevertheless maintain a commensurate sense of dramatic irony to bridge the gulf between the real and the fabulations of the imagination, between aspiration and fulfillment. It is easy to deceive yourself without the ironical sense, easy, for example, not to acknowledge that one can be said to possess something only when one has lost it and one's loss can also be one's gain. Some things to be seen in their real value, only to be seen at all for that matter, when all personal and active interest in them renounced. Yes, enact, dramatize yourself. To examine the matter coldly and logically, like a philosopher attempting to resist the enchantment and deceptions of language, will entail spiraling into solipsistic drivel, as if one could ever finally escape being the dupe of language.

Yes, there is no escaping it, the truth will out somehow, what is not said will be said, all will be exposed, all betrayed sooner or later. Confess all, be honest with yourself, even if it all descends into self-deception, fumble around in the dark in your forest of questing questionings and see where all this takes you. Perhaps only then will you begin to understand something and – who knows? - even become intelligible to yourself and to know yourself. The strength to risk all must be taken. Even if you don't know anything, better to talk with a brick wall, or like Saint Anthony with the fishes in the river, than not talk. Nothing like real conversation, again even if only with yourself. Better than nothing, and you have all the time in the world, when it comes down to it. Despite it all something wants to be said, even if someone has turned off all the lights. Words written, words outside living dialogue as though carved in stone only mean what they mean, no argument, no appeal, all dead weight, silent. Speak then, speak real words, with your own breath. You may well even profit from this monologue, or rather dialogue with yourself, and perhaps in the end it will not be so useless after all. What is sometimes more enlightening than such periods of idle conversation when today I barely get time to hear myself think? Socrates, after all, preferred conversation to the lecturing and hectoring monologue. Then set everything else aside for a few moments at the very least. Sometimes it is best to let things happen by themselves and grow in their own time, like the famous flowers of the field. The age of heavy industry age is drawing to a close, there is no doubt about that. It is gone already, I should say, and good riddance to it. Such frenetic energy is pathological, too much gets done, there is too much activity nowadays, we are burning the world up, burning ourselves up. The hardest thing nowadays is to do nothing rather than something, and harder still to listen to oneself. Now that so much is behind, after the old longings and illusions extinguished, the old deaths dead, yes, perhaps now is the time to speak and risk the mockery of the silence, time to address the infinitely blue otherness of ocean and sky and retrieve from time lost those fragments, those moments gone but nevertheless mine, the only things I can call as such, mine precisely only because lost, because not mine, my guiding star. All of this must be rescued from the past or it might never have happened.

Perspective, it's perspective you need. It's time to see your own past at one remove as you might the past of another, of a stranger. A stranger. Yes, even having said this word 'stranger' already I feel better, already I could be on the right track, and I could well be on my way out of these endless thoughts. The idea that I am both my past and not my past, both what has happened to me and the one reflecting on what has happened, is appealing and makes sense. Yes, that is good. Already I feel less alone, and the thought itself is almost enough to turn me into someone as if newly born, summoned into being from nowhere, with a past, with a history to speak as though of another's, with memories, some good, some bad. I like the idea that I can see myself as another and look down on myself from high. And if in this darkness I am indeed alone, how can I be said to be so when the very act of having pronounced 'I am alone' already implies, with elegant irony, that I am not alone and there is always another even if I think I am alone, such a pronouncement already drawing towards itself as if by a magnet a clamour of swarming otherness, crowds, multitudes preceding me through the ages. So not so alone then as you had thought, no, never alone. There is that to be said for reading: at least you know you are not as alone as you might have believed.

These books mounting up in stacks, read and reread in your search for your Absolute, as you so grandly call it, yet still nothing proven, no love in your heart and the others laughing behind your back at such preposterous endeavours. Time, I think, to put aside books for now and leave off reading these philosophers endlessly contradicting each other, unable to agree on anything and leaving me none the wiser at the end of it all. What has happened demands a response I was not yet willing to give it and, again, without this response the question will not leave me alone and blight everything. Yes, get to the bottom of it all once and for all. All these cheap doubts are a bad habit, a misuse of reason and knowledge, mere sophistry, distraction, abstraction, a whittling away of time. Set aside all such cleverness and trickery in this search for what is undoubtedly nearby if not staring you in the face, no doubt so obvious in retrospect it would barely require any special knowledge to see in the first place. Act. Yes, once and for all, after the endless wandering and vacillation, the shunning of imperatives, the devilish proliferation of possibilities you know you can never actualize, begin somewhere, face yourself, recollect, take stock. At least be courageous enough to see yourself for what you are and forgive yourself for what you are not, for what you don't have, and choose this definite time and place against an infinite number of choices and possibilities. Take up where that stupid, spotty Hamlet left off, entangled in his own tortuous hesitations with his 'to be or not to be' and all the rest. Here at this windless and barren island, the granite mountains soaring into the grey, maddened clouds, start from the present, from here, at this point on the earth's surface, and even if you are nothing then that is at least something, something you can say about yourself despite everything, something to remark on, to snatch from out of the air, a way to regain your bearings. That I am human should at least account for something (and if I am nothing could I also be everything?). Although there is much to be said against the species and however it often pains me to count myself as a member of it, there is no use beating yourself over the head about it, no point in complaining. Such sordid recriminations will get you nowhere.

No, this won't do, it won't do at all. Return to the absolute, return to your obstinate theme and try to connect the dots. Its menacing darkness won't go away, everything comes up against its question, it faces you, and unless the question is taken by the throat, unless all this is articulated, formed and named nothing will amount to anything. To begin with then, what is this absolute, this black rock of all being, what do I mean by the absolute, what is all this absolute business anyway? An absolute what? Is it an absolute Knowing? Or is it indefinable, perhaps recognizable by its absence, affirming itself when denied, revealing and concealing itself at once, unreachable, mocking every attempt to name or picture it? Impossible then to resolve this directly, to knock the bastard off.

Try analogies, pictorial, picturesque, colourfully poetic, as befits depictions of the heavenly revelations, the celestial visions of former days? No, nothing so grand, and apparently such days are well gone anyway. Better something closer to home. Like the glimmer, yes, return to the glimmer, the unassailable glimmer. Remember that moment when the truth in its Edenic simplicity and clarity spelt itself out in capital letters, remember that paradise perhaps still here in the present smiling out at us unbeknown to us, as in the old legends of the simpleton hero who discovers that the thing he set off on long journey to find was, after all, at home all along. It wasn't, as I recollect, anything beyond or above the world, nothing remotely and mystically abstract, but rather imbued with the resplendent precision of the intelligible, a body of knowledge so physical you might almost touch it, a body at once as close and familiar as one's own and yet as foreign as that of another's. And what else? Oh yes, the uncanny convergence of the universal and particular, the comical collapse into each other of the unearthly and earthly, and also those delicate, discrete things, tenderness, the intimate charm of the prescient suffused with the glow of eternity, those once demeaned things given meaning again. All this unfathomable, wanting focus, but nevertheless suggesting that all was not in vain, that there was yet something to hope for, the celestial cornucopia of the future almost at hand, the garden of the world once more pure and habitable, unassailably innocent, freed at last of the obscure malevolence poisoning it and everything as it was before the snake appeared. An absolute, yes, and not someone else's but my own absolute, waiting for me, my magic castle, my own Holy Grail, my philosopher's stone, but perhaps, in the end, not that at all but only your face, Stella, your blessed face theatrically wreathed with flowers in the framed photograph of you I used to hang on the wall.

That's it, this will do now for the things I want to resurrect of those happier, gentler days, lingering, joyous moments inviting you to abide with them forever in that land of youth and truth. Truth or knowledge are worth nothing if not joyous, if not ecstatic. But again, all this is meaningless unless understood. Only with such understanding can I cure the old stake-in-the-heart wound. Lying here, sinking into my inert body, the rumbling ocean waves below and these babbling, muddled thoughts spoiling everything, serving only to distract. The thing is to get to the heart of the matter and examine why you lost the plot. It is time to face up to it all rather than try and forget it ever happened.

But perhaps only with peace and quiet will I find a few tentative answers, no matter how vague, that reveal themselves in their own time and their own way, without this grasping and unseemly clamour. But there are no signposts or maps. What else to do then but stumble on, even at the risk of losing the plot? Yes, spirit of eternity in your limitless benevolence, with all the time in the world on your hands, I will abandon the shelter of my little room and its not so splendid isolation and strike a deal with you: show me a few sights, lead me on a magic journey, show me the life that has passed me by, the one they all told me about. Risking everything, I will allow you to lead me on a merry chase if only for the sake of making some slight sense of it all. Lead me up the garden path if need be. I am always one for pretty gardens.

But still the confusion, the obscurity, the incoherence. I am getting nowhere, my thoughts falter, disperse, I'm loosing it. But is all this complication, this dialectical argument even necessary? After all, it's harmony I want, the sweet agreement of all things, as in the old days. It is only words that provoke argument in a way that the world of the senses does not, and philosophers are always at odds with the world and with what they see with their own eyes. Time then to take a walk to clear the mind. Enough of sitting still. I'll cross the lawn to the sweeping, epic beach, and there is nothing to beat the quiet perfection of this fine sunset with its silken array of colours. Walking is the best way to resolve things. You can think epically, expansively, without restriction. After all, the old philosophers Kierkegaard, Nietzsche and Rousseau said they had all their best ideas walking.

How much in the beginning did it seem that the world was all your own, your own empire, your magic realm wrapped in the immense cocoon of a child's dream and you were a 'king of infinite space.' Needless to say, all this quickly changed and now it was a matter of myself versus that world from which I had been estranged and about which I now realized I knew so little. Who then was that 'I' then and who is this other 'I' who lives through me now? The question 'Who are you?' perhaps even the wrong question, the wrong question from the beginning. Am I one person, nothing but a first person singular? Two, of course, always two, never only one, and the very spirit of contradiction itself, like everyone else. Am I not always another, both an 'I' and someone I might barely recognize in a mirror or photograph? A ridiculous idea to be identifiable only as a single entity, a self-enclosed, discreet, rounded whole. One would be smothered by the *Iness* of the 'I', weighed down by it if one weren't so divided, there would otherwise be no dramatic conflict, no impulse or longing to cajole me from the womb of unknowing into the blessed sunlight of transparent consciousness. Without such a lively dialectic where would I be? Yes, sometimes I am happy to converse with myself, as happily as I might converse with another, but of course such solitude can easily reduce one into talking gibberish. Perhaps then I need a patient interlocutor, or better still a Mephistopheles, a devil's advocate, a friend in enemy clothing, a harsh, unforgiving critic to clear away all those old ideas to unearth the truth, someone to bring me back to earth from these maudlin meanderings, these vain dreams and speculations which can only remain abstract if they are not made concrete and part of myself. Either that or I will get nowhere and fall on my face yet again.

Still the question, though: if I can never return to that little patch of Eden, my own Eden and no one else's and it is barred to me forever, how will I regain that heaven (all these Biblical metaphors and images are useful) surely promised to me, the one to which all the signals seemed to point, the heavenly Eden without which this brief interval rounded by a sleep would surely be senseless and pointless? Where would time's brave progress lead me without such a thing? Surely it cannot merely be a matter of the bad forever turning to the worst, an endless fall from that eternal moment into time as mere succession marked by the ticking clock? What earthly sense in that? Only last night, in a state of half dream between sleep and waking, an image of my own childhood shimmered into view against the colossal blackness. It seems that I had journeyed to the city of my birth and, with a shock of homesick recognition, found the place where I would play as a child. I saw that empty yard edged on two sides by the towering brick walls and the white stucco summerhouse and deep green latticework fronting the shrubbery at the far end, the Loddon Lilies and sycamore trees partly obscuring the brackish river further beyond. I had to ask, looking at this spectral image of myself: Who was this infant in all his promise and confident innocence and who has he grown in to, who ought he have become and is now clearly not, and what does time and its accumulation of memories between then and now amount to, what story has been left off, untold? As is the way of things a seed duly grows into a plant and blossoms or bears fruit, but what have I grown into, what is the result of all that busily prolific, patient growth? I am a shadow of what I could have been. What then to do about all this, where to go now if I have indeed lost my way like poor bewildered Dante wandering recklessly in the dark wood?

It's true, admit it to yourself, I have been wont to brush others aside as no more than walk-on figures. But perhaps, as the old monks would say, it is wise to remember that even the most unwelcome and boorish of guests can indeed be Christ in disguise. I often tell myself that it is useless to expect much from people, that I don't need others. I like to suppose I am the heroic master of my own fate but am I not yet another of those modern souls confined to their own little plot of space pressing in on them, entrapped inside their infernal, eternal solipsism, reasoning themselves to death, living their lives inside their own skulls, and unable to decide on anything, to choose this way or that?

But it could be that fate does not, as they suppose, lay waste to everything and there is indeed such a thing as destiny, a lively destiny that shapes our ends. Perhaps all will come out right in the end, time will heal all wounds and all will come out in the wash. Yes, I might well be on the right path without knowing it. Then is it all finally an unknowable, unsayable mystery, even to myself? Perhaps better if I am beyond even caring if I don't know. To remain a mystery to myself may at least preserve intact this one thing against a world which would like to know and explain all, to preserve truth in formaldehyde. And yet again am I not also searching for a sense of clarity and was it not exactly because, afraid as I was of destroying the spell of that precious moment, I did not seek to address and clarify it that the question still pursues me as unfinished business? I have allowed myself to cherish its memory nostalgically as one does a favoured piece of music yet without extracting its ultimate significance, without asking myself why it had its singular effect on me, what it was saying, what it meant. And without analyzing what it was trying to say I do not even know what it is I am lacking, what it is I do not know. Yes, if I am not to look back at my own life with regret or repugnance for lost opportunities it is important to revisit the event that set me off on this attempt to hold the world in my hands.

Again, set aside all feeling and try to look at things more carefully, even if indeed feeling should be all. A philosopher presumably concerns himself with ultimate concerns such as ontology or teleology and not the price of groceries or the world gold market. He is popularly assumed to be wise and knowledgeable, able to resist the enchantment of words, but realizing after all these years how little I know about anything I am the last person anyone would come to for wisdom and truth.

But Stella? Where are you in all this?

It's detail, it's names I want. It is not as though I had no more than otherworldly and universal matters in mind. Like anyone else I am conscious of the marvelous uniqueness of one individual and I can appreciate as well as anyone a discreet object such as a tropical flower in its blaze of colours, I am one for great magic vistas of land and sea and I observe as closely as any physicist the varying formation and collapse of waves on the sand.

A word, a sentence, a question, perhaps even an image? An image then. Here, somewhere I have some coloured chalks. Take them and sketch a picture. A picture is worth a thousand...

So done, what do I have? A towering black mountain and, superimposed, the spectral image of a blue, no, a blood-red rose dispensing its heavenly scent, vertiginous petals suspended in permanent, luminous stillness.

Stella. All this reminds you of Stella. Stella, then. Did it all start from here? It is twenty years ago now since you first saw her. How quickly the years have gone and how blurred, how insubstantial that time seems now. But there has been no one remotely like her. Your own *visione amarosa*. A face and place from long ago.

At certain moments you see the world for the first time, you like to believe you were granted some kind of infinite knowledge, you like to believe you figure in one of the world's great romances. Such as that spring night in the garden park, for instance. Yes, I remember the circular clearing in the trees with the lunar light of the globe lamp at its centre, the festive stars, the carnivalesque stage flowers, daffodils, narcissi, tulips, azaleas braving the cold absence of sun, her voice, the night air sharply harmonious, everything electrified with new life, the celestial and earthly sounding one chord, attuned to the same song, all truth self-evident. I had never seen more clearly, never been more lucid, the vagrant, gabbling old ghosts and demons banished forever. Since that time glimpses only, obscure promises, evanescent intimations that one day such magic might return like the second coming. Sometimes, during one of my pointless ambles, every street, every unpromising corner and confining horizon reminds me of what seems both lost and yet somehow also in front of me, untouchable, unreachable like the ancient gods we all know and love but who perhaps have not disappeared but are still with us, in hiding. The magic castle is still unfound, love nowhere but everywhere, an absent presence.

Should I stop this fruitless nostalgia? Don't look back, it is said, don't be Orpheus. Look what happened to him. Torn to pieces. Shouldn't I then make an effort to venture into the world and, as they say, fall in love again? No, to look for love now in that way would merely be chasing the same thing all over again, repeating the same mistake and there would be no end to it, and there's no doubt that I misunderstood love and approached it impetuously and artlessly, and no wonder it has returned to avenge itself on me. Yes, that was what happened. It's the same old story. Love and loss. Novelists, poets and musicians make their living from it.

Suppose I surrender to the moment and act, doesn't this entail living, like any grand romantic, only for the immediate moment?

No, examine the past, retrace your steps. Something must be made out of this, ask yourself how it began, think now, speak, enough hiding from yourself in the dark. Yes, it was one bland and hopelessly perfect day when you were reading and writing in the study, your great endeavours going nowhere. An Easter Sunday, I remember now. That holiday, that holy day to mark all other days. A band playing at the roadside, a small party underway, twenty or thirty people, I remember, and not being able to shut the music out, and despairing of everything anyway, I decided, to hell with it, I would abandon everything and join the real world with all its noisiness. Wait... don't I still have her photograph somewhere? Yes, here it is. Even now, with the embarrassed detachment of hindsight, I can see that I wasn't blind, that love is anything but so, and she was, as one would say, beautiful, no denying it. Certainly, others thought not so beautiful at the time. Pretty maybe, but then each to their own. That was when I saw her for the first time. Or was it the first time? Hadn't I seen her somewhere before? She was standing on the other side of the road with a small group of her contemporaries, students no doubt, three women and two men, I think it was if memory serves correctly and all this is not a false. She was about nineteen years old. Looking away from them, she gave me an ambiguous, Mona Lisa kind of smile, open and innocent yet at once somehow ironical, in a way to suggest that we already knew each other, and moreover already knew what we were each about to say and barely needed saying, everything already having been said in that faraway, unknown country, that other life, that other happier universe we alone had somehow issued from together. I recall clearly enough now: yes, I was the wanderer who, in a distant, strange town on the other side of the globe, and as if in a dream, meets the one who was destined for him after being unaccountably lost over the years. Easy to mock such sensations now. Notwithstanding the explanations of science that such phenomena are matters of biology, of brain chemicals and hormones, and can make no claims for unique and permanent significance, could such a thing be doubted at the time? It goes without saying that such amorous encounters are nothing to write home about. There is nothing original in all this and yet it would be commonplace of me to belittle such feelings only because they are recognized by everyone without exception. Mock love and it will destroy you. It is through love that we enter the mythological realm of the gods and goddesses, so all this is not to be sniffed at, it is not a laughing matter, it is not a mere entertainment or distraction.

So then, that was it, a glimpse only and she was gone, like Dante's young Beatrice seen for a few heaven-storming moments in the sunny piazza, and no matter where I looked I couldn't find her. No one, not even the students, knew where or even who she was. But as is often the case with such matters, only a week later, by the unaccountable machinations of fate or chance, and after I had given up the search, we did see each other. And yes, rather than coincidence, I like to think it was fate or destiny. If we had been searching for each other in the hope we would meet, how was it that I finally saw her at a place I would not normally have visited? What were the chances of that?

Yes, it had to be destiny, I am sure of it. I remember the magic, otherworldly details of it all: following that second encounter, it transpired that we had a mutual friend who, in his ambisexual role of Hermes, finally brought us together once again and from that time on I like to think we were in love, as they say, and I certainly told myself so, having already heard and read about this love business before and determined to see what it was all about. Needless to say, for five years we lived together. Were we happy? In retrospect, it would seem we were both happy and unhappy in equal measure. And was there a marriage? No marriage. But why then did we not marry, why did we not stay together? And what story might I tell myself about this? But this would be the kind of story of no interest to anyone, a story told too many times before. Enough to say we separated and, presumably, parted ways forever (But then again, who knows? Perhaps I may yet see her again, in this or another world.). I left her or she left me. So let that be the end of it. I wanted more than love could offer, and something primal in me wanted the impossible: perfect union, fusion, communion, the human and real-life equivalent of that previous vision of harmony and unity. She standing in her own glory in The Paradise Garden and surrounded by acres of flowers. So preoccupied was I with the great Universal, with the Universal Whole, it's little wonder I didn't see what or who was staring me in the face. But how does one address a singular being of supernal aspect and origin, how address someone who had been dead many times and learned the secrets of the grave, and had been a diver in deep seas, and for whom all this has been to her but as the sound of lyres and flutes? Despite one's purest intentions, one is simply reduced to the level of babbling idiocy. Always easy to mistake the woman for a Goddess, a fabulous figure from a dream, unreal and played out as in a story or play. How could you expect anyone to embody such perfection, that perfection which it is our tragedy to conceive yet not attain? The mere act of seeing and touching a goddess, even if she does not know she is a goddess, is enough to obliterate anyone. There is no way one can match her with a commensurate power and be worthy enough to touch her hem. Yes, I wasn't quite 'all there,' anyway, always absent, absent from myself for that matter, my head in the silver-tinged clouds. How could I bring her happiness when I was no one in my own eyes, and I had robbed myself of any sense of self by my own abdication of that very self for, I thought, her benefit, or rather not for her benefit but, I should say, in the hope of losing that self in such fantasies, not having found that kind of happiness I was still hoping to find in others but which can only be found, if at all, independent of them? Nevertheless, having parted, did I not have the horrible sense that I had in some way murdered someone or rather, I should say, murdered something in myself? Perhaps I saw myself then as a kind of poet, and being a poet could excuse myself of any number of sins. Wasn't it I who created a wall between us, didn't I leave her and in so doing surrender the promise of happiness only for the sake of scribbling lyrical, sentimental effusions over such losses? All this, no doubt, out of fear when you realized that if you are not to contaminate the other with your own impoverishment you must serve the beloved out of the munificence earned for oneself over the years. In the end it might have been better if you had stayed with her. Then you may well have learnt something. But if only you had spoken when you should instead of holding silent out of some misplaced sense of holy quietude! Damn it all! After all, we only know each other, if at all, through conversation, through pretense. I asked myself questions silently and incoherently but did not voice them, afraid, no doubt, to break the spell, to disenchant ourselves with the truth. And who, indeed, knows what unwelcome secrets we may have found? Make the darkness give up its secrets, always question, always refuse to accept ignorance.

But these constant, needling questions, this vacuous big 'no' to everything: all this is tiring. Am I to be nothing but the perpetual denier, negator, questioner of myself, my own best critic? And you often say: I merely want the reconciliation of the old opposites, the perfect harmony of the spirit and the sensual and so forth. At heart I am no contrarian sophist, not one for answering a question with a question like the philosopher I am supposed to be, not one for the perverse pleasure of questioning and arguing for the sake of it. Certainly, I ask questions out of dissatisfaction with the 'what already is,' yet the thing I want is the big Yes, the big, rollicking Affirmation. This absolute has a certain colour and also a necessity without which the world outside will remain drably monochrome and insufficient.

And yet could it be that this long fall from grace, which everyone at the time found comical, is a blessing in disguise? Without this beastly Felix Culpa would I now be asking the questions necessary to bring all this to the light of consciousness? Yes, mindful of the others who had came unstuck in the big bad world, I could have stayed home, but then where would I be now without such forwardness and excess? A complacent, self-satisfied bourgeois would be the answer. You were told the great truths, certainly, but at the time they meant nothing and so you had to find them for yourself the hard way, alone. And there is something to be said for such youthful romanticism. Those shoreline vigils by the rocks under the moonlight when you would gaze yearningly like Shelley or Novalis up at the lightened window, for instance. Perhaps such moments were the beginning of a path to the truth, perhaps in hindsight those youthful, Byronic romances in all their reckless naivety weren't as silly as they would later seem in more sober, disillusioned times. Despite their intemperate and fleeting nature they were trying to tell me something I was deaf to, bound up as I was in this infatuated idolatry of a single being as the very image of the cosmos, the cosmetic of the cosmos. Sad to think about it now, about the great what-might-have been, the failure of all that seemed to then lead to some glorious, impossible possibility. But perhaps it had to be this way after all. You weren't ready for the full incandescence of love, there was too much yet to know of the world and too much to acquire before you had anything to give.

Yes, it is necessary not to confuse the transitory with the permanent. "Things, like joy, also yearn for eternity. Things do not merely want to be themselves, to be 'the thing-in-itself,' but always more than they are, always in excess of themselves. Yes, it's true, children are better at these things, they understand illusion, symbol, theatre, the pretense necessary to deceive and seduce one into truth. 'Except you become a child can you see the kingdom of God, etc....' Diotima, the midwife in The Symposium, had it right all along, yes, she knew firsthand what Socrates and his drunken cronies didn't, she, familiar with birth and propagation as she was, well knew that Eros is not so much a god but love itself and the principle of relation, the relation between the I and the You, the sensual and the spirit, the transitory and the eternal. Beauty, she tells us, is an image of the good inspiring the inception of new life from the old in the effort of the good to preserve itself for eternity against the transience of things, and I should know all that. What havoc, then, we cause ourselves in our impossible hopes for total fusion with the mystery of the Other when we renounce the good as the antagonist of the aesthetic and sensual! I see it all now in all its demonic innocence, its thoughtless immediacy.

But all these abstractions, this unnecessary self-reproach, these regrets, this casuistry, this looking backwards all smell of the lamp and nothing can come of it. Such an attempt to make an account of oneself before others cannot hold and I am only digging myself deeper into a hole. Nothing can be changed and perhaps, anyway, all has been determined, plotted from the beginning, written in the sky and all is for the best, all for the good and it isn't a tale told by an idiot. Things happen, things end; events, people, loves: they come and go.

But still, where is she now, I wonder? Most likely somewhere perfectly happy without me, I should think. Who knows? It would never have lasted, anyway. And if we ever do meet again no doubt we won't recognize one another. All that another world away, the dark ages, and yet shadows, shades, echoes follow me.

But what is the point of this elegiac and futile foray into the past, this shameless confession, this tedious anecdote which strikes so many false notes? Only perhaps that although we never had children there was a birth of a kind, that an iridescent phoenix did, after all, rise from these sad ashes, a hope, a resurrection you could say, a perpetual impulse beyond all reason for what might be.

Yes, it has to be said again, I must admit it to myself: like any child I want answers. This pure light endures in the void, and what are all hesitations, doubts, arguments, calculations and stratagems against it? It persists despite them. Meaning, yes, there's no point in denying it, I must find meaning, if only for myself. There is a pattern, an order out there, out of focus, staring at me, and without such meaning, even if words are powerless to formulate it, the world's devilry will play cat and mouse with me and I will be everyone's fool, the plaything of fate and circumstance, the dupe of language.

Answers. But yet again, do I fear them, as some fear their own wishes coming true? Am I afraid to answer my own questions? Is that it? And even if I were to find the grand answer and clear up the mystery once and for all, like a detective, should I infer that everything would be solved and I could henceforth counter every argument thrown at me? But then what? What would be solved? Little enough, I imagine. And then again is it only answers I am looking for and would I reduce for this purpose everything to rule, to systematic explanation? Perhaps I prefer mystery after all, perhaps there is only mystery and nothing else and everything is, indeed, ultimately unknowable. And is this Absolute something that already is, a being, a thing, or is it rather less a presence than an absence, a black void within the knowable, within the very horizon of knowledge, and perhaps even death itself? Or love? Is it love? Is that it? Yes, I had always suspected as much. The extraordinary magic of a singular love. Perhaps I have set the stakes too high, set unnecessary obstacles and only now am beginning to learn something. But if philosophy would reduce everything to prose, already I am breaking its rules and, damn it all, this is beginning to sound too much like poetry. But then again, perhaps it is poetry I am after. Abstract nouns such as the absolute, beauty, love, joy and so on: almost meaningless, dry husks of words we hardly know what we are saying when we use them, words marking the very line where ignorance begins. Poems in their own right, you could say. They are what they are. Sometimes they seem to have a meaning, sometimes not, but nevertheless charming crystals you can peer into and see afar, empty and yet somehow acting on one with a force of their own. Grand words, indeed, and yet how I miss grandeur, the grandeur of the good old days!

All I do here is wait, with only these idle musings for company. If only grace would descend like a dove, as it should if there were any justice! Having achieved nothing, as usual, here I am merely staring across the English garden out to the very un-English infinity of blue porcelain sea and sky. That Baroque marble bird bath supported by its three frolicking but helpful cherubs. I have liked it since early childhood. How did it ever get here? Again, disjointed fragments, no coherence, no sequence, no meaning here, there or anywhere. A distant passenger plane (a 777?) ascends over the sea into the child-like blueness. To where? South America? Australia, Europe? All this traveling. Are they going home or going away to unknown lands? But perhaps, like everyone else, I was born to travel, I am a traveler, a traveler and nothing else, perhaps a time traveler, perhaps time itself is transporting me to some distant land and I am heading somewhere without knowing it. Perhaps that was your original error: to place yourself at the centre of everything when you would have done better to see yourself less as a centre, less an atomized being surrounded by other atomized beings, than a direction, a direction in time. Yes, that is certain, there is no denying it, no spiriting away the mystery of time, our very substance, indeed our breath, our heartbeat. Without it everything would crumple and pile itself up and there would be no measure to things.

This much I know: that I am here, nameless, a body positioned in space or, no, rather a body in time, in the vast dimension of time. Sometimes I am not at home in this meagre world of three dimensions where people awkwardly collide, brush past one another and separate again, I could well be a perpetual exile here not knowing whether I am coming or going, and yet in the more generous and forgiving fourth dimension of time am I not always myself, with at least the freedom to choose this or that, to be anything and anyone? Could time itself be the angel of my redemption, leading me to eternity's ink blue empyrean, my true home, my promised land outside time altogether? When it comes down to it am I not, in the end, a creature of this sleek, insouciant eternity in love with its creatures, could I even be the substance of eternity itself? Yes, eternity resolves everything. There is a kind of perfection there, a resolution, an adequate end, with all time on my side, all the riches of eternity in store I would have nothing to loose. Such an idea is at once both appealing and discomforting, yet somehow validating it all. Yes, I could almost live with this, it would be a way out of this endless business. Unconfined by space, released from subjection to its categories, as I lie here in bed, my body weightless and forgotten, I am commensurate with myself, I coincide with myself, I seem to have what might pass for dignity and freedom, I am king of infinite space, if only for a few moments and with no bad dreams. Yes, space merely weighs me down, encircling me with its invisible, changing boundaries, in space I am all gravity, but eternity has no such restraints, no such boundaries, there is nothing to come up against, never an end to anything and no tearful partings.

Or could it be that I am afraid? Is that what it all comes down to? But afraid of what? Of being alone? But how can I think I am alone when there is always you? What am I without you, Stella, what do I have to speak of and write home about, what can I even see and know without you, what would a singular and undivided self like me be without you but a prisoner within a mirrored room of endless reflections of himself? But then who are you? Where are you?

Yes, I believe it's all coming back now and everything has not been lost, if it was even lost to begin with. I swear I am reaching the heart of the matter and beginning to understand something at last after this endless pursuing and grasping and perhaps it hasn't all reached a dead end and my search has been necessary after all. The spirit of this absolute that once visited me is the very balm to its wound, the search is the search for the wound's own cure for itself. Yes, I already have the sense of myself as less than one amongst others, each relative to the other, and that what I have been looking for is an absolute not outside or beyond or above but none other than my own tangible self, or rather an absolute 'I' contained by this self, its vessel, its opening, its window on to it, an absolute not fixed but incomplete and constantly becoming. Yes, that's it, I think I see it now, I could stake everything on such an idea, I should have known it all along, it has a certain weight, a neat logic, it is an answer of sorts, an exit. 'In my nothing my All shall be found.' Nothingness then no cause for alarm now. With such understanding I can feel again, like King Anfortas the wounded fisher king, cured of his affliction at last, joy declaring itself to the shining, silent nothingness, all his Christmases at once. From such ideas I believe I could make for myself a world fit to live in again. Yes, it seems obvious. How well children know such things. The absolute dissolved and transcended at the very point touched, I have failed, the absolute dead, so long live the absolute and back to square one again, coming full circle, the goal and origin in one. What more to be said beyond all this? Too much explained and explained away. No need to spell things out. What left then? Only the glimmer, the soft glimmer in the dark.

It's time, I think, for another walk.

The Big I

It would seem that it has announced itself, cold and hard in its unconditional demand. If you haven't been to heaven, you don't know what you're missing.

Labyrinthine perplexities and doubts, spleen and melancholy surrender to this brilliant white sun, this C Major chord shattering the Minor chord tonality of yesterday from where, emerging as if from the land of the dead, you have ascended vertically thirty-two thousand feet over the world's calamities and meanderings into these open pure skies where all seems for the best and all as it should be. Surprised with a new sense of plenitude and adequacy to yourself, the world at your feet, you brim with a near Messianic, childish impatience to embrace the world's intense abundance you see spread below you, because yes, at last, after your aimless, circular plodding, there is no doubt that you have glimpsed the famous Good Place they always told you about.

At the risk of madness you would try to lend it the words that would save you from its dumb enchantment, but what then can be said about it, how, in your autistic rapture, can you speak of it, how to give wings to something which is nothing? If unsaid its whispering, garbled message will be lost if you cannot find such words, it knows something you don't know, there are questions to ask of it and, in your perplexity, you want to ask what it is you know when you know it, what it thinks, what it tells you, what you see through its eyes. In contrast to such unforeseen, precious, unsurpassable moments, how familiar and how many more words lavished on them are longing, desire, disappointment, unknowingness, loss, absence, languor, ennui, the handy, constant themes of poetry and fiction, the bad news that goes to make history, and is it not time such moments had their own say in the order of things, even if the darkness which has had its own say for long enough still presses down around you? Transitory, aerial, no sooner here than gone, yes, but more than a consolation or temporary reprieve, this time it is too intractable in its claims on your regard to dismiss so easily as you return to your workplace .

Yes, this time, unwilling to allow this brief period of exquisite clarity to pass by like a dream, unexamined, unquestioned and un-acknowledged, you are resolved to sound its very depths, to grant it the kind of attention you might otherwise have reserved only for matters more grave and substantial, and you would like to allow it to tell its own side of the Big Story, to speak on its own terms and in its own time of what only it can know and dreary melancholy only dream of. Once, in an earlier day, perhaps from youthful arrogance and bravado, you disregarded this identical moment of miraculous plenitude streaming endlessly from its bottomless cup, dismissing it as an inconvenient disruption of your own precious equilibrium, an affront to your own fragile self-possession and reassured yourself that, anyway, as it was already above words and beyond understanding, and there were already far too many explanations foisted upon you nowadays, why bother posing it the question of what it was and meant? It was what it was and nothing more, and was it not, you reassured yourself, perhaps no more than a temporary restorative from the world's demands, an idle fantasy, an empty play of forms to distract yourself from the dead ends and unresolved contradictions impeding your famous constant search for the 'real and the true?' And yet a question mark dangled in the air and you surmised that perhaps it was not the mere effect of a random cause, a simple re-lief from a vague discomfort, the kind of empty euphoria following a narrow escape from some ordinary misfortune or danger, and that its visitations, barely recorded and outside of history, without a his-tory or story of its own, a mere parenthesis in the world's affairs, might advance a more profound kind of knowledge, a broader reserve of meaning than both unhappiness and simple happiness? The unhappy moments are quickly forgotten or suppressed and as for happiness, happiness comes and goes, a ripple on the surface soon to leave everything as it was before, unchanged and untouched, but this new influx of joy raises more questions than it answers, it explodes the old order, opens new, infinite vistas, rearranges the landscape and, you could even say, chemically alters you for good.

The rule that prevailed before no longer holds and the old preoccupations, the intractable quandaries and doubts of yesterday seem and like mere child's play now. A more spirited, supple kind of logic comes into play, if you can call it logic, a sinuous, Baroque, Italianate, playful, gestural line of argument unafraid of divagating from or recoiling on itself, unafraid of the unexpected and extraordinary; an outlandish comedian barges in to undermine fate and expectation, to violate the laws of cause and effect, to alter and redeem that past which now, in retrospect, seems a mere preparation for this moment to which all the wrong turnings were the right ones conspiring in their own way to lead you. Not a cock and bull story after all, it seems, and at last the world, only yesterday drowning in its ocean of waste and shame, is once again a shining clarity and goodness, the lost Eden restored to itself, a smiling, childlike sun burns every grey vestige of doubt and melancholy to cinders, the world is at your feet and you are filled (stupidly so, some will tell you) with the promise of a magnificent and impossible future in store.

If it is endlessly precedented in literature, art and music it is nevertheless yet also unprecedented and unique when it addresses you directly by your own name. Transformed, jolted in an instant from a merely passive observer of circumstance you realize that you are infinitely more than the arbitrary and battered entity, the sum of your own history you once took yourself for.

What then is this new, transformed, unique self that inhabits you? Are you no more than the plaything of a mood or delusion any psychologist would only be too happy to rid you of? Surely, they will say, it cannot last, it will consume itself and when the effects of its narcotic wear off what you thought was yours forever will slip away and leave you to face the dull facts once again. But rather than any obscuration or blindness is this new 'I' not more down-to-earth, more clear-headed and objective than it ever was, the very spirit of lucidity itself, its magic lens bringing everything that would otherwise remain blurred into crystalline precision? Your own defense against every joke the duplicitous world would play on you, you are not blindly naive, knowing less than those who, more solemnly austere, supposedly possess a higher kind of knowledge, you have not escaped into some anonymous and impersonal ecstasy. No, you see yourself clearly, you are resilient, neither humbled, secluded or excluded, you celebrate and envelop rather than oppose the mystery of things, and how then unlike former times when everything else beyond, if it was not at the ready disposal of your own will, could only be an obstacle or enemy. How laughable seems that crude combativeness with which you would erect impregnable walls between yourself and the world in a fruitless effort to ward off whatever might threaten your precious happiness, that happiness which yet secretly yearned for the limitless spaces and chance intrusions of that neighbouring Otherness that, to preserve itself, it was obliged to exclude. Never the fool of irony, you revel in the ancient song of opposites, of stone and water, light and darkness, earth and heaven, the aesthetic and ethical, artifice and nature, you makes play, make hay with contradiction and paradox, it no longer bothers you that one thing is also something else, a self its own other, presence absence, repose movement, substance nothingness or truth falsity.

It is overflowing with more order and significance than it knows what to do with, it is full of itself and seems to know everything that matters, it has all the strength it needs...but for what? How to contain and activate this influx? Rather than take permanent residence in some private heaven, rather than hold onto this gold which will otherwise only turn to lead if you guard it to yourself, there is only one thing to do: descend like an old prophet from the Himalayan summit you have flown to and initiate the world into this newly found magic of yours. The media brandish the bad news, we have the 'great and burning issues of the day' to consider, flags to wave, causes to address and against all this they dismiss it as vacuous, frivolous and of no interest, its implicit, naive assumptions baring no relationship with the way things are, and yet by what absolute measure do they, handling the word 'utopia' with embarrassed quotation marks like surgical tongs, discredit its claims? What they, in their solemnity, take for callous naïveté, to you is is merely the arch irony of experience replete with the regained purity and clarity of childhood, the smiling wisdom of that goddess Sophia who is more knowing than any of the sages put together, and freed from anxiety towards the tenuousness of your attachments you are flush with a new generosity, infinitely compassionate towards that suffering which, sometimes despite itself, you well know yearns for well-being. Once, in an earlier life, in your own yearning for the infinite, you would abandon the transitory and particular to side for the great pure realm of universal ideas, but why now would you spurn this earthly world for such a realm when you already comprehend the whole in all its parts and you are already the very substance of the stars? Rather than by any eternal Platonic ideas you would measure the value of any claim to meaning only by the authority of this single, momentary foretaste of utopia, this standard par excellence around which all meaning and value must constellate, this essential element that any philosophical system must accommodate if it would avoid spiraling into meaninglessness. But if the heavenly utopia is indeed dead, then long live 'utopia,' and the wings of these quotation marks resurrect the word, embody it, give it new life, new flight.

Is it only transitory? But the moment festively consumes and exhausts itself for the redoubled joy of endlessly begetting itself and reveling in its own transformations, and even if all is as intangible and provisional as an image or dream you feel that as the true mystery is not in the hidden depths but the visibility of things it is enough to touch the world with the eyes.

There are, you well know, only two seminal plots, two narratives in any life, namely the successful passage from birth to metaphorical death and rebirth or else their refusal or failure, and less easily satisfied with negative sensations of insufficiency or absence to stimulate your ambition or inspire you with your ideas and images, and wearied of constant doubt and prudent self-weighing, wearied of sequestering yourself behind the walls of this darkened room, you are tempted to abandon your pile of musty books and to act, to surrender everything to fate, to step outside and throw your lot in with the world, and because you know very well that the course of life would be without plot, symmetry or shape if it were not for this vital second birth when, distinct from everything universally innate, you come into your own and become who you are, namely your own creation, you want to undergo time's transforming alchemy for the Big Chance of your second birth. The narrative others told of you may have everything to do with them, but why should that be of your concern? Let them portray you how they will, let them gossip all they like, you have yet more to tell, more surprises in store for yourself.

If you breathe the rarefied air, if you are quite at home with immensity, you do not exclude the simple charm of the local and particular and celebrate as much as anyone else small, immaculate things, sinuous arabesques, all that counters the powers of the brutal, everything which would diminish the bright clarity of the day's mystery. With this happy marriage of infinity and the particular the universe seems to dissolve into cosmic laughter, into a cosmic joke akin to that celestial Nitrous Oxide, that primal laughing gas which, we are told, instantly negated the void at the origin of the universe to ripple outwards and bring all form and substance into being. Laughter is, indeed, the only exit from the endgame of reason and logic, the joke the only short-cut from A to Z. The world, once intractably heavy and remote, is lightness and transparency again; everything dances and flies, concurring and resounding of its own accord.

In the end, whatever the case, it is too late to undo it. Better, as they say, to leave the dead to the dead. Why disturb their sleep? It is a predisposition latent in the natural order of things and the dice is already loaded in its favour. There's no stopping it.